SUNNAH

MALIK SALAAM

DEDICATION

For the woman who challenged my beliefs…
And the children who made me stand by them.

Adapted from the screenplay, SUNNAH

I created this story for anyone who has ever struggled with belief. For those who search for The Most High in their actions and pray that they are truly judged by their intentions.

IN THE NAME OF THE CREATOR OF ALL
THINGS…

SUNNAH

THE OPENING

It was her smile. It flooded me with serenity. I knew it was something she rarely shared. Nothing perfect in its delivery... a consequence of not enough practice. But, all of a sudden, time slowed. And settled. Our connection was the only thing that existed. And I searched for the words to acknowledge the moment. There was one salutation that could express my appreciation...

"As-Salaamu-Alaikum," I mouthed.

I understood she considered herself a free spirit... not confined to a particular ideal. Her actions resulted from of what she accepted as truth. Right and wrong did not hinge on punishment or reward. Her beliefs were stripped of traditional structure... no special handshakes... or loaded greetings.

She held up two fingers, "Peace."

I believed her. She wanted ease for me... more than I had ever wanted it for myself. And then...

A gun shot!

The sensation of peace escaped me. I grabbed onto the emotion as life slipped from my body.

I've had many near death experiences.... ignored their severity. Glazed over them as a part of life. Lessons lost on battlefields.

But as the first bullet ripped through my torso, I realized the occasion was unique. I felt closeness to My Creator.

The pain tore me from her eyes. I don't know if I had ever appreciated their detail. Chocolate- with soft gold flecks. Mosaic in design. And without flaw.

I prayed... begged my Lord to allow me the image of her eyes in the afterlife...

A second shot!

My life played out in an accelerated rewind. Reality intensified as my years compressed into fractions of seconds... raced past me. I saw my choices as if they weren't mine. I was a spectator in my existence.

I turned toward the blast... there was a different set of eyes. Less warm. They danced with paranoia and malice.

A third shot!

My flesh burned... A piece of my rib cage shattered... the warmth of blood filled my lungs.

Most stories about dying include memories of floating into eternity. The bright white light that draws you in. But that wasn't my reality. My body was on fire. I was being torn from this world. And in the distance- a small light glowed... bright crimson.

CHAPTER ONE

1.

The red light from the stereo held Young Mustafa captive. He tried to block out the sounds surrounding him. But the noises were all consuming. The loud commotion distorted sound. Young Mustafa was trapped in chaos.

The red glow gave him a focal point; allowed him to be both inside and outside of himself. And his surroundings seeped into clarity.

It started with the sounds closest to him. Ummi's recitation. A prayer. The slow, precise rhythm of the Arabic language. He didn't understand the words, but the emotions behind them reverberated urgency. The whimpers of his two younger sisters exaggerated the vibe.

"Sandra come open this damn door before I kick it in!" Somewhere- not so far off- Abu hammered his fist against wood. His threat was real.

The fights weren't abnormal. The noticeable difference was Ummi- a top-notched prized fighter- hiding from battle. Her fear created a much more dramatic contrast.

"Mustafa."

He wondered if it was his mother's first time calling his name.

"Mustafa," Ummi said it again, "go answer the door for your Abu."

Young Mustafa got up from his kneeling position. His body became heavy; his legs transformed into anchors.

Ummi urged him on, "Go ahead, now."

And he went... stood at the bottom of the stairwell and stared up towards the kitchen. He was too short to see the front door. An arm clawed the air. He was sure the limb belonged to Abu, but it didn't ease the horrific sight. He looked back at his mother... She was in the middle of another prayer.

Young Mustafa gathered himself and lifted his foot onto the first step. His breaths intensified.

The second step...

The urge to pee rushed his bladder. He didn't have the best track record for controlling his piss.

The third step...

Mustafa saw a portion of Abu's 250-pound frame squeezed through the chain-locked door.

"Sandra," Abu's screams subsided as he caught the glimpse of Young Mustafa from the corner of his eye.

"Mustafa," his father's tone changed, "Come open the door."

The little boy stared across the kitchen.

"Son, don't let your momma's emotions scare you... come open the door," Abu's voice carried with it comfort and truth. They were instructions for life. And Young Mustafa followed his father's command.

He drug his body across the vinyl floor- stared at its design… shapes connected and collided into one another. Still overwhelmed by his task, Young Mustafa convinced himself that if he kept his head tucked to his chest and lumbered forward everything would be okay.

He reached his destination. Abu sucked his flesh out of the crevice. Young Mustafa pushed the door shut. He took a deep breath and slid the chain off of its latch.

Before Young Mustafa cleared his path, Abu barreled inside. He flew through the kitchen, and hurled himself into the basement.

There was more screaming and banging. But Young Mustafa retreated to his safe space. Certain words pierced through his walls...

"Motherfucker…."

"Istafullah…"

"Fuck you…"

"Allah says…"

Young Mustafa watched his two sisters scurry up the steps into their bedroom. There was more knocking and shouting. His feet cemented into the floor. He wanted to leave… run to refuge. But at six, your parents' home is supposed to be your place of comfort. Young Mustafa had no escape.

Two shadows charged up the stairs- chasing after one another.

Abu made it to the front door. Ummi stood in the basement doorway. Mustafa was stuck in the middle.

"Akil, if you take your ass out this house… you better stay over there!" Ummi's voice seethed with so much anger it demolished Young Mustafa's thinning wall of security. The words sounded absolute.

Young Mustafa tried to understand the convoluted message. Not five minutes ago his father, exiled from his home... struggled for entry. And once in, he rushed to escape... ordered not to return. Young Mustafa couldn't make sense of it.

Ummi continued her declaration, "You think me and my girls need this... we don't need you."

Young Mustafa wondered why he wasn't factored into the equation.

"Nigga, do you hear me? I swear Akil, you leave out of here- you keep your black ass over there."

Abu turned on his heels. His face stewed with rage. The fighters were ready for another round. "You can't tell me where I go... You don't decide my rights," he barked.

"Fuck your rights," Ummi woofed back.

"Istafullah." The statement came from deep in Abu's gut. The word always sounded disgusting to Young Mustafa even though he didn't comprehend its full meaning. But he knew Abu used the word to describe the worst things imaginable. Abu walked closer to Ummi and growled, "In Islam..."

But Ummi wasn't in the mood for a lecture and she cut Abu's statement short, "Islam... His/slam, nigga," Ummi moved in closer. Her teeth clenched as she uttered, "I don't want to hear that shit. You don't tell me how to believe, motherfucker! I'm tired of you and your self-righteous ass! Get the fuck out of here!"

Their eyes' sizzled with rage. They had squared off...

And Abu folded. Backed away. He seemed frightened by Ummi's words. Young Mustafa had never seen his father back down from anything... had never witnessed a look of fear in Abu's eyes. Ummi moved in closer.

"I mean it... Get out," she snarled and grabbed a plate off the buffet. The shatter of the glass onto the vinyl floor startled Young Mustafa. Ummi became hysterical, "Get out! Get out! Get out!"

Young Mustafa had never heard such a sound. He looked at Ummi wondering what she would do next. Her skin, the color of sunlight, had turned blood red. Her fist balled tight by her side.

The little boy cut his eyes toward his father, but Abu's pupils had turned to stone. He stood motionless. A joint getaway didn't present itself as an option. Nothing in his father's eyes promised salvation. Nothing in Ummi's tone guaranteed safety. Young Mustafa was stuck in a burning house. But he couldn't hear the fire trucks in the background.

Outside, a car's engine roared, and the sound of rubber screamed across concrete. It was over.

And as soon as Ummi realized it, she ran to the door. "Akil," she cried out to his tail lights.

But Abu had vanished... and part of Ummi left with him.

She lingered at nothingness, dropped her head, gathered the last of her strength, and trudged back into her home... or what remained. Young Mustafa maintained his position. Dead still. Hoped he was as invisible as he felt. Ummi walked right past him.

And Young Mustafa was alone.

2.

Mustafa opened his eyes. He stared around the room. It was empty. The feelings from his slumber carried over into real life. And Mustafa longed for company… wished the people from his nightmare would come back to rescue him.

But 20 years later, and Mustafa was still alone.

Mustafa shook off the haunting thoughts. He looked over at the other side of the bed. The steel black .45 lay beside him. She was the only girl that shared his bed. Her touch made the ghosts unimportant.

Mustafa grabbed the pistol and pulled himself upright… double-checked to see if any jinn were bold enough to hang around now that he had a hammer in his hand. He chuckled at the thought of such comic mysticism.

"Bismillah," Mustafa whispered. He stood up and placed her on the dresser. And then dropped to the floor…. catching himself as his face was an inch from slamming onto the old hardwood. Each push-up jammed the ghosts deeper into their boxes. He counted out one hundred repetitions.

Mustafa finished his workout and moved onto wudu. He washed his body in the way of The Prophet. The way billions of Muslims had done for over 1400 years. His morning was regimented. Mustafa followed the path of Muslim Men. He believed all parts of life fit into a proper place and time.

His small shotgun house sat on Lawton St. The old pine floors creaked. The mortar on the walls held heat in the summer and cold in the winter. Each room led into the other. The house was dark- despite the time of day.

Mustafa's prayer room was nothing more than a small rug and a wooden stand that held his Quran from touching the floor. Mustafa entered, gun in his right hand and a string of wooden prayer beads in the other. He placed the pistol on the ground next to the velvet rug, and wrapped the beads around his wrists.

"Khakhamah to salat... Khakhamah to falat," Mustafa chanted. *Come to prayer... Come to worship* were the orders. Mustafa could feel millions stand with him. He adjusted himself to them... *Shoulder to shoulder and toe to toe.* Mustafa could hear his Imam say, *close in the ranks, Believers, to keep Iblis out.*

"Allah-hu-Akbar," Mustafa proclaimed... God is The Greatest. He reminded himself of his Lord's Mercy and Forgiveness. Begged for Allah's guidance in *ruku* (standing), *qiyam* (bowing), and *sadjda* (kneeling). Prostrated in perfect order.

Mustafa finished his salat and unwound the dhikr beads from his wrist. He chanted of his Lord's Graciousness, and His Mercy, and His Greatness. Repetition ruled Islam. Every practice served as a reminder of what Allah had bestowed on Mankind. Mustafa embraced the rituals because they kept his spirit tamed. He even incorporated it into his language. Sometimes the mere utterance of *Subanallah* or *Mashallah*, rescued Mustafa from deviance.

Mustafa opened his closet; his clothes maintained in the same structure as the rest of his life. Shirts and jeans on hangers, grouped together. The colors muted. Mustafa believed Muslim Men stayed away from flash. No red or pink. No gold or jewels.

Mustafa stared at his wardrobe- even though one choice wouldn't be different from the other. He grabbed a pair of starched jeans. Threw on his crisp black t-shirt. And slung the white and black checkered keffiyeh (scarf) around his neck.

Mustafa adjusted the tool in his waistband and made his way to the front door. He put on his black Nike boots. Raised on a diet of five prayers and a yearly fast, Mustafa had principles engrained into his psyche. One of his rules was: no shoes in the house. Mustafa didn't believe in tracking the world into his home. He laced up his boots.

Mustafa bowed his head for one more dua before he exited.

"Ameen."

Mustafa was ready for war.

CHAPTER TWO

It was one of those mornings when the energy in the police station felt like a locker room. State championship. Game on the line. And the Boys in Blue brought home the trophy.

Detective Zimmer surveyed his teammates. He sipped his cup of Joe and basked in the energy he created. He had made the big play.

Zimmer, a raging narcissist, assumed most people were beneath him. He had maintained his cornerback physique. He had an uncanny ability to understand the criminal mind. The style of an international drug lord. The charisma of a world-class pimp. Zimmer's life was a never-ending cycle of being present in the right place at the right time.

Captain Harris walked in and nodded at Detective Zimmer. The Captain's large frame commanded focus. The entire room scrambled to find order. Cops topped off their coffee and grabbed a few more donuts before they took their seats. Zimmer maintained his position.

Detective Thomas observed the exchange between Harris and Zimmer. He quickly redirected his gaze. Thomas didn't want to get caught eyeballing his partner. He recognized Zimmer's need for attention. And Zimmer would mistake nausea for adoration.

Thomas wasn't jealous of his longtime partner. He knew first-hand the whole *Captain America-bit* masked an inflated ego. Zimmer couldn't give two fucks about serving or protecting; he adored the shine.

Thomas found satisfaction in riding his partner's coat tails, but he didn't trust Zimmer. Thomas knew if Zimmer's self-image ever felt bruised, he'd attack without rules. Thomas didn't want to be on the receiving end of Zimmer's wrath.

"Aight, settle down," Captain Harris bellowed, "There's a few things we need to get to." Harris waited until each officer's eyes were front and center; dumfounded that these were the people selected to enforce justice. Most of the men were meatheads with little ability to form a free thought.

Harris put on a pair of reading glasses and cleared his throat. He read over the notes from *the people upstairs*. Same routine every day... and every day closer to his retirement. He cherished the thought of not having to lead the supposed shepherds- who disciplined the sheep- to slaughter.

"Okay... so yeah," Captain took a deep breath, "We need to keep an eye open for bootleggers. DVDs... knock-offs... you know, anybody without a license to sell goods. This is illegal, and The Department is tightening the reins. These neighborhoods with walking traffic... Get out those squad car." The room shook. "And lets write those citations... and make arrests. We need to see more activity in this area. And I guarantee... as you turn those stones more trash is gonna surface..."

"Bootleggers, Captain?" Sargent Simmons spoke, out of turn, for The West End. He knew if it came to his guys having to hop out of their cars, Zone 1 would fall short on the unspoken quota assigned to this sudden crackdown.

Harris took off his glasses and stared in Simmons's direction... or maybe right at him. Harris had a slow eye and a thousand-yard stare. A less than lion-hearted man shied away from eye contact with The Captain.

"Yes, sir... I'll make sure we are on top of it," The Sargent tried not to sound as belittled as he felt.

Captain Harris let the uncomfortable silence linger so that everyone felt it and then proceeded, "And last but not least it's not often I hand out congratulations for doing the job we're obligated to do. But I love it when we one up the feds. So, I want to give a round of applause for the leader of our homicide division... Detective Zimmer."

Zimmer took a sip of his coffee to hide his smirk. He examined the room: a few officers snickered. Their jealousy pleased him. A few others turned toward Zimmer- excited to be associated with the superstar. He loved these moments, but his humble facade shielded his delight.

Captain Harris finished his statement, "His amazing work led to the arrest of that militant fanatic that took the life of two of our own..."

Protocol flew out the window; an eruption of applause, whistles, and screams interrupted Captain Harris' statement. The space returned to its locker room glory. Zimmer waved off the wanted attention. Thomas clapped the hardest and the loudest.

Zimmer wondered if his partner harbored some deep seeded resentment for his constant success. Zimmer couldn't imagine having to stand in his own shadow… much less that of a lesser man's. The thought of his partner wanting his limelight, made Zimmer's victory even more special.

Captain Harris raised his hands to settle the room, "Which brings me to my next point. Despite what we think of that cop killer, The Imam has a lot of respect in the West End, and helped to keep the neighborhood in a certain 'order'. So, make sure you tell your men to keep their heads on a swivel out there… No telling what could pop off."

Harris' statement had a sobering effect on the officers. To say Imam Yusuf had respect in the West End Community was an understatement. A more appropriate way of saying it was the West End belonged to the Imam.

Imam Yusuf first made his name during the civil rights movement as Huey Jackson aka Hue Jack, a fiery speaker and a militant leader. He was infamous for coining the phrase: Violence is as Amerikkkan as Disney World. He authored a socio-political piece called Niggers Die. In his writing Hue stated, *he could honor no laws that didn't have him in mind when they where created.*

Hue Jack gained the attention of a cross-dresser named J. Edgar Hoover, who framed leaders of the Black Power Movement. Jack was accused of criminal activity and placed on The FBI's Most Wanted List. After his capture, he was convicted of armed robbery- a common charge assigned to people from The Movement- Hue Jack served 5 years in prison.

The years behind bars transformed Huey Jackson into Yusuf Shakur. It was his release and relocation to Atlanta where he founded The Masjid Al-Ruh, which meant The Holy Spirit and became its spiritual leader or Imam. Imam Yusuf owned a local grocery called The Neighborhood Depot. And helped to shape the West End Community.

It was a well-known fact that Imam Yusuf didn't allow drugs, prostitution, or gambling in his neighborhood. The ban on illicit activity was a tall order considering the West End occupied a small corner of the Westside... a sector of Atlanta steeped in the inner-city blues. The streets of Lawton, Holderness, Lucille, and Atwood neighbored Ashby, MLK, and Stewart Avenue- notorious for all the things the Imam outlawed.

Only so many miles could be covered, but the blocks that circled The West End Park was off limits. If Imam Yusuf could sit on his front stoop and see you, you had better be doing the right thing. And word on the street was if you were doing the wrong thing, the punishment went from zero to severe- real quick. There were tall-tales of shoot-outs with drug dealers and violators being blown up in their car... Lethal force for violators of Imam Yusuf's laws became Westside-folklore.

For those that believed the fairytales, when TV's around the country broadcasted: BREAKING NEWS: IMAM YUSUF SHAKUR FORMERLY KNOWN AS HUEY JACKSON KILLS DEPUTY, they accepted the hype. Those people didn't take it as a shock that Imam Yusuf was on the run and the FBI's Most Wanted List for the second time in his life. It was easy for them to believe that he had fled out of guilt to Alabama, where they captured him and his murder weapon.

But for a larger part of the West End Community this charade reeked of a government conspiracy. It was another complicated attempt at dismantling their community and targeting their leadership. Members of the West End weren't passive, and that meant- just as Captain Harris said- *anything could pop off.*

"Okay," Harris checked to make sure the severity of the statement had sunk in, "all right… dismissed."

The officers filed out. Ready for whatever came their way… and if it didn't come for them, they would, definitely, come for it.

CHAPTER THREE

The room was well lit. Sunlight diffused through the incense smoke, and created a soft glow on Ayanna's mocha complexion. Scents of jasmine and sage filled the room. Ayanna had turned the sitting-area into her sanctuary. And every morning she sat in stillness, concentrated on her breathing, and searched within herself for a connection to The Oneness. She inhaled. And exhaled. Lost herself in the rhythm of her breaths.

Ayanna James was previously known as Anna James-granddaughter of a sharecropper… daughter of a mother suffering from bipolar disorder. Anna never accepted the fate of her life or her environment. As a child, little Anna needed to cope with her mother being different and emotionally unavailable. Anna found an escape in books. Her alternate realities began with Jody Bloom and grew into Veronica Decides to Die and graduated to Toni Morrison and Sonya Sanchez.

After high school, Anna attended Howard University and studied sociology. She thought she wanted to be a lawyer. But Washington, DC was a chocolate city with a rich culture. She was exposed to art and poetry. An internship at an inner-city community center helped her realize her need to rescue children.

Ayanna's work in the non-profit sector alerted her to the injustices of society and the mis-education of Black people. Anna *shook loose* her old skin… She, even, changed her name to Ayanna. In Arabic the name meant beautiful flower, which attracted Anna because of her longtime connection to nature; not to mention it was no secret that she was gorgeous. But the Hebrew translation solidified Ms. James' choice for her new identity. The name meant He answers.

Ayanna had never been one for traditional religion. Raised in a catholic household, her Grandmother forced little Anna to attend Catechism. But Ayanna discovered other beliefs as her scope of the world expanded. And she learned to listen to The Voice from within, instead of hunting for a God outside of herself. And without fail, whenever she searched within, He answered.

Yoga and meditation weren't common in Ayanna's hometown of Jackson, Mississippi. It was a small two-lane town, where women worked at the casino and men labored at the State Penitentiary. The thought of gluten-free or social activism were foreign concepts to people raised on a diet of pork and taka vodka. The simplicity of their lives never called for protests or riots.

Ayanna allowed her eyes to open organically. She unfolded her legs from the Lotus position, stood, and stretched her petite frame skywards. Meditation created peace and she took a moment to plan her next step.

Her downtown loft was an open airy space, which let in fantastic light during the day, and at night the glimmer of Atlanta's skyline was mesmerizing. She painted her walls with earth tones. She stocked her bookshelves full of literature ranging from the metaphysical to the fictional ideals of feminist *sheroes*. Walker and Zora. Nikki and Shanga. African statues and amethyst rocks served as bookends. Fresh plants and potted herbs hung in the corners and lined the windowsills.

Ayanna glided through the living room towards the kitchen and filled her ceramic teapot with filtered water. She decided against turning the pot on, in case her shower ran too long. The last thing she wanted was the teakettle screaming at her early in the morning. Ayanna knew she had a finite amount of time before the peace of the morning was replaced by the chaos of real life.

The scalding water, from the shower, sprayed onto her body. She lathered herself with organic black soap that she purchased from the health food store. The shower swept Ayanna into another level of euphoria. The sensation was orgasmic. Ayanna lathered the precious space between her well-sculpted thighs. She felt the urge to massage her clitoris. But she refrained.

It had been awhile since Ayanna made time for masturbation, and even longer since she indulged in the real thing. Her vagina throbbed. And it was only a man that could ease her angst. But the exchange of sex bought with it the exchange of energy... the footprints of lovers and their lovers past. Ayanna didn't have time to entertain males who refused to be men.

And more important than satisfying her urges, was the peace the universe granted her from sacrifice. Ayanna used the peace as armor and identified it as strength. Her fasts and rituals created a quiet corner in a chaotic mind.

Ayanna walked back to the kitchen- her small robe clung to the water, still drying on her flesh. She turned on the tea. It was time for her to start her day. And right on queue her cellphone made a beeping sound. It was a text.

Ayanna hated how technology created 24-hour access to people. A phone was an electronic leash. And carrying a honing device didn't sit well with Ayanna's free spirit. But she was, also, of the world. The nu-hippie. Equipped with flawless knowledge of pop culture, technological trends, and new age mysticism.

Ayanna checked the message: THINK I WANNA GO TURN UP TONIGHT. The message was from Yasmeen, Ayanna's best friend.

Ayanna shrugged at the thought of a bar filled with Atlanta's pretentious implants. Her and Yasmeen often disagreed on what the terms of *turnin' up* entailed. Ayanna responded: WE'LL SEE.

She knew she had no intention of going, but she hated to blow her childhood friend off. Ayanna was smart enough to know that a person is only awarded so many lasting friendships in a lifetime. And she understood those relationships required selflessness.

Ayanna escaped back to her bedroom and started the process of getting dressed. It took a lot of work to put together her look. In magazines her style was classified as *boho-chic*. Long flowing outfits. Bold patterns in earth tones with splashes of citrus. Layers that created a modesty and then for contrast, the slight sexy reveal of a midriff or the peak of a shoulder blade.

Ayanna took her time in the architecture of her flair. The clothes piled up on her floor, and through a technique of elimination a she made the final selection- just in time for the whistling of the teakettle.

Ayanna turned off the pot and seeped her tea. She pulled up the flyer she had designed the day before. Ayanna- along with millions of people across the nation- watched the manhunt for Imam Yusuf Shakur.

Ayanna was *afro-centric*, and watched the unfolding of current events under the scrutiny of a Black microscope. She paid attention to the words unsaid and the evidence of things unseen. The accusations of Imam Yusuf's involvement with the murder of a police deputy were full of holes. And for Ayanna truth was always solid.

She tweaked the flyer and saved it to her thumb drive. Ayanna found pleasure in her quick reaction. The world was consumed with superficial distractions… trinkets and illusions of freedom. Ayanna's soul was from another time. And, although, the fight for her generation was different, Ayanna still believed there was a fight to be had.

Ayanna centered herself before leaving out the front door. She was prepared for battle.

CHAPTER FOUR

1.

"I'm good, baby," Mrs. Johnston, a regal elderly Black woman, announced from her front porch. "How you doing this morning?"

"I'm aight," Mustafa responded politely.

"You know," Mrs. Johnston walked to the edge of her porch, which was an indication she had something more to say. "The Lawd work in his on way, baby."

"Yes ma'am," Mustafa obliged Mrs. Johnston's attempt at comforting him, "You good, dough?"

"Baby, every day the Lawd let me drag dese old bones out the bed I'm blessed," Mrs. Johnston put her hands on the small of her back. "Gotta git myself down to tha store and git some Goody Powder for my arthritis... And some Coca-Colas. Chile I tell you."

"I can go get that for you Mrs. Johnston," Mustafa offered.

"Whew, baby, dat's so sweet of you," Mrs. Johnston retrieved her money out of her bra. She was grateful to not have to trudge through the August sun for her necessities. She added another item to the list, "And get me a couple cans of salmon- so I can make me some patties."

Mustafa waved off her money, "I got it."

Mrs. Johnston reflected on the enormity of the gesture. "Ain't nobody thinking 'bout what dem news folk talkin' 'bout," Mrs. Johnston scoffed.

"Yes ma'am," Mustafa smirked.

The frantic beating on a storm door followed by desperate screams interrupted the intimacy of their exchange. "Aye Rico... open da damn door, man! C'mon Rico!"

Mustafa pinpointed the sound to a house two doors down. The house had always been an eyesore. White peeling paint. The front lawn trampled to dirt. Cars parked in the yard.

But the Junkie banging on the door first thing in the morning was evidence that things were further out of order. Mustafa diverted his attention back to Mrs. Johnston who stared with worry at this glitch in her morning routine.

Mustafa wondered if Mrs. Johnston's hand cupped her heart out of worry or if her bosom just seemed like a comfortable resting spot, after replacing her money in her safe space. Regardless, the stance intensified Mrs. Johnston's look of unease, and for Mustafa the image sparked a sense of responsibility.

"Lawd know some thangs dese eyes get tired of seein'," Mrs. Johnston turned back toward Mustafa, "Dat's why dem folks didn't like tha Imam... He policed his own... Y'all gotta keep up that work."

"Yes ma'am," Mustafa looked back at the Junkie banging on the door, "Let me get outta here... I'll get that over to you."

"I'm sure you will, baby," Mrs. Johnston smiled and went back to watering her flowers.

Mustafa stayed fixated on the Junkie. He couldn't believe the audacity of what he was witnessing. He wanted to run up behind him and pistol-whip him into submission. But for Mustafa it was not the time. He was aware of the eyes watching The West End. There were no police in plain sight, but the smallest altercation could have APD painted into the picture- like they had been there the whole time.

As Mustafa got closer to the house he saw the details of the transaction. A looming figure now stood outside with his shirt off and his underwear on display. Mustafa couldn't hear the conversation, but everything about the interaction was wrong. Mustafa's glare was intense; he waited for eye contact. Even when the Junkie scurried past him, Mustafa never broke his gaze on the dope boy.

The dope boy put away his money and his bomb of dope. He checked his surroundings... And he saw Mustafa staring in his direction. The two locked eyes. It was the first step in their confrontation. Mustafa flared his defined nostrils, and the dope boy responded by spitting on the holy ground.

The confrontation had escalated without a word being said. Mustafa kept the dope boy in his sights; turning his head so the dope boy comprehended Mustafa's gaze was purposeful. The dope boy never looked away, which further infuriated Mustafa.

Mustafa ran through the chain of events that lead to such a blatant act of disregard. The dope boys on the Westside understood the rules. There was no crack being sold around the perimeter of the park... within walking distance of Al-Ruh. Nobody within the eyesight of Imam Yusuf would dare *serve* in broad daylight. Those things took place on the other side of Ralph David Abernathy.

Mustafa had to be strategic in how he handled the situation. He didn't have the luxury of going to sit on the stoop with Imam Yusuf to receive clear guidance. Mustafa had to reason this one out on his own.

As he stood at the top of the hill that led into the park, he realized, more than ever, his crew would be looking toward him for leadership. Mustafa was ready for the challenge. He made a small dua before he walked onto the basketball court.

2.

"I'm tellin' ya, Akh," Reek's wiry frame was always extra animated, "dat hijab wasn't hidin' nuthin', Shim."

Reek tapped Shim on his shoulder. Touching while talking was a tool Reek used to keep his audience locked into his conversation. "Every time she moved- I'm like, Mashallah, dis could be my third wife."

"Dat mean you'd have to take proper care of da firs' two," Mustafa stated as he appeared onto the court.

Reek heard Mustafa's judgment from behind him. He suppressed his normal reaction to somebody *trying him*. And let out a snicker, "Oh, you got jokes."

"If dat's what you wanna call it," Mustafa rarely joked. He greeted his other two comrades.

"So, you heard anythang else 'bout da Imam," Shim asked. Shim was a gentle giant. Large but humble. A bear no one wanted to see wake from his slumber. His mind was simple and he didn't understand the intricacies of small talk.

Mustafa took a breath and looked around almost as if to make sure nobody was listening in the empty park, "Naw... Bro. Abdullah called me last night, but you know he ain't sayin' too much on nobody telephone..."

"I'm tellin' you, akh," Reek didn't need anymore information, "we gonna have to bust him outta dere... Real talk."

"Bust him outta where... prison," Saif blurted out, "Reek what da hell is you talmbout?"

Saif, the most ruthless of the bunch, had a short fuse for foolishness. Him and Mustafa came up *from the mud*. But he never learned the mechanisms for patience that Mustafa had developed.

Mustafa met Reek in Fulton County Jail, while he was fighting an attempted murder charge. Reek was in jail for an unrelated armed robbery. He was innocent, but because Reek ran with the crew, who committed the crime, he sat in jail before he would snitch.

Mustafa introduced Reek to Islam. And when Mustafa caught beef with some young Gangster Disciples, Reek was right there at his side. Mustafa beat his charges, and Reek ended up going to the chain gang. But Mustafa was loyal, and when Reek got out Mustafa brought him into his crew.

Soon after Mustafa came home, Saif had to do 3 years for a gun charge. Technically, with Saif gone, Shim would have been next in line, but Shim wasn't the sharpest crayon in the box. And Reek was nickel-slick. So, by default, he gained more leverage in the crew.

Saif never liked Reek. Saif wouldn't acknowledge it, but he was jealous of the bond that Reek and Mustafa developed behind the wall. But Saif viewed jealousy as a weakness. So the only thing he dealt with was the facts on the surface: Reek was a loud mouth, who was way over the top with his religious judgment and just as excessive with his immoral behavior.

Saif only cut for the authentic. His connection to Islam was in his blood. Saif was born and raised a Muslim, and he separated that from his survival.

"Jihad, Akh! What is you talmbout, Saif," Reek retorted, "Subanallah, I'm sayin, shawdy, we gotta stop talkin' and roll some heads."

Saif glared at Reek. He ran through the many ways he could end Reek's life. But Saif's bond to Mustafa kept Reek safe. Mustafa saw the flame ignite in Saif's eyes.

"But in da real world we got some real problems," Mustafa interjected. "Saif, you know 'bout dis dope house up on Holderness."

Mustafa knew Saif stayed in the loop, and his connections in the underworld were vast.

"Dat white house. Yeah, I know da nigga who run it from back in da day," Saif recalled, "Rico... used to run in da Temp. He set up shop since we been layin' low."

"He ya people?"

"Hell naw... run his mouth too much." Saif cut his eyes toward Reek. "But on some real life recklessness, ya dig?"

Reek had checked out, as usual, and missed Saif's jab.

Mustafa processed the information. Rico was a live-wire. Mustafa and his crew were gangsters… strong enough to go toe to toe with whomever. But amongst killers, Rico was one of those guys who enjoyed destruction.

"What we gonna do?" Shim was ready for orders.

"We ain't gonna do nuthin'," Mustafa contemplated, "not right now."

Saif and Shim both understood. Reek didn't hide his agitation.

Mustafa understood that sometime Reek required more explanation. He tried to offer Reek something constructive to do with his energy, "Keep your eyes on him, Reek… We'll get to it. Patience, Akh."

Reek hated to wait, but he felt like he had bumped heads enough for the morning. And he was ready for the meeting to come to an end. So, he chose to nod in agreement.

"Aight… Me and Saif gotta go handle dis other business. 12 gonna be hot today." Mustafa looked to see if he statement summoned the devil. "Da last thang dey gonna wanna see is some big threatenin' Muslim like Shim walkin' da streets. So, low visibility, feel me."

Mustafa tapped Shim on the shoulder. Shim understood the truth in the joke. Black men- in general- but definitely of Shim's physical stature evoked fear. And fear was the root of violence.

CHAPTER FIVE

Levison's office was nondescript- a testament to his business practices. Elusive. A blur between ethical and profitable. A few file cabinets. A huge desk and a bar. No degrees on the wall. No volumes of self-help books- encouraging losers to be successful. It was unclear what business Levison conducted.

"Gertrude," Levison called out to his secretary, "I am expecting Mustafa this morning and…"

"And I will notify you before I buzz him into main lobby," Gertrude completed his statement. She detested the random visits from Mustafa. And Gertrude didn't want him nor *the one with the crazy eyes* to linger. Gertrude wasn't positive what Levison's dealings were with the dangerous duo, but she was sure that whatever the two touched turned into trouble.

"Thank you, Gertrude," Levison found it hilarious that the old Jewish lady disapproved of his clients. Levison was a businessman, and his aim was to acquire property that was profitable. And he had no qualms concerning the source.

As Levison continued with his morning, Mustafa and Saif made their way into the downstairs lobby. Saif eyed the security guard as they signed the guest book. On the elevator Mustafa and Saif made the corporate folks uncomfortable. On the thirteenth floor they exited the elevator and strolled to the end of the hall. Mustafa rang the buzzer and looked into the camera, mounted in the ceiling.

Gertrude called Levison and alerted him of the insurgents. Mustafa searched for patience as he waited in the hall. Just as he was going to press the button again, Gertrude buzzed him in. Mustafa and Saif exchanged looks as they made their way into the office's waiting room.

"Good Morning," Mustafa was polite.

Gertrude didn't return the greeting, "Mr. Levison is ready for you."

She pressed the buzzer that opened to another hallway.

Mustafa smirked at Gertrude's silent judgment. Saif saw nothing amusing in her actions. Mustafa led their trek down the hall. They stood at the door and were buzzed in for a third time.

Mustafa could feel Saif tense up every time the buzzer sounded. Saif didn't like the noise of the buzzers; it reminded him of the two years he spent down the road. But more than the similarity to prison he hated dealing with Levison... Saif was against those who opposed Islam, and Levison's Jewish beliefs- no matter how loosely practiced- were a red flag.

Mustafa and Saif entered the office. Levison held up his index finger as he finished up his phone conversation, "The prices are as low as they are going to be, George... Exactly... One man's tragedy is another man's triumph... Okay, Buddy. We'll talk."

Mustafa and Saif cut their eyes. They understood Levison's greed. But business- like war- was not always righteous.

"Muh," Levison blurted out as he hung up the phone, "Good to see you, my friend." Levison partly stood and extended his hand.

Mustafa was always taught that white men shook hands because their business dealings were shaky. Black men- when doing business-shared a firm grip. The slight difference symbolized a grand distinction.

"Saif, I see you're in your regular chipper mood," Levison jostled.

Saif's silence was thunderous. He flared his nostrils and shot two Molotov cocktails with his stare.

Mustafa shifted in his seat. He knew that Saif wouldn't intentionally loose control when there was money on the line, but he also knew that Saif had a short fuse for *the khafir* (disbeliever).

Levison felt above, whatever, harm Saif carried in his heart. Levison smirked at the thought of *street justice*. He redirected his attention to Mustafa, "So, what do you have for me?"

"What you got for me," Mustafa countered. He was also bothered by Levison's egotism.

Levison chuckled as he reached into his desk drawer. He liked to test the limits. Every thing for the seedy businessman was a power struggle. Levison was a big game hunter, and he liked his prey to fight back. He tossed an overstuffed envelope across his desk.

"You know," Levison started his pitch; "it was really difficult to get your asking price for this last job."

Mustafa grabbed the envelope and thumbed through the collection of Benjamins. He could eyeball money the way a seasoned drug dealer could eyeball weight or how a chef knew the right measurement from sight and touch.

Mustafa handed the cash to Saif, and Saif stashed it in his waist... on the opposite side that he carried his pistol. He then pulled another pouch from his pocket. Saif handed Mustafa the sack and Mustafa tossed it onto Levison's desk.

Levison squinted at the bag; he and Mustafa shared the talent for poker faces. But Levison was as excited at the contents of the pouch as Mustafa was about the paper tucked in Saif's waist. Once his excitement was in check, Levison pulled, from his desk, a black velvet board and a jewelry loupe.

Levison dumped the clusters of stars onto the midnight sky. He examined the jewels. Levison tried to conceal his grin at the amount of carats rappers put into a single piece of jewelry. And how they then paraded those obscene symbols of riches amongst wolves.

"Muh... can I be honest with you," Levison didn't wait for an answer, "In this business you have to know more than the customers you... acquire your products from."

"You wanna be more clear," Mustafa scoffed. He despised being confused for a dummy.

"In a sense, that is what I am referring to," Levison tried to hide his fangs. "The clarity of your last batch was a little cloudy. Now because I consider you a friend..."

"We ain't friends," Saif had reached his tipping point.

"Whoa there, Saif," Levison was at the ready, "No need to get all Gaza Strip on me, Brother."

Mustafa glared at Saif. And despite Saif's instinct, he followed Mustafa's instructions. Levison noted Mustafa's control.

"I just want you all to comprehend," Levison continued his lesson, "that most of the jewels that the average *rapper-homie-yo* buys may not really be worth what they paid for it."

"Dere's a surprise," Mustafa could've guessed what Levison would say next.

"Now, I have a 'connection' that happened to... uh... mention in casual conversation, a more educated consumer that is coincidentally a client of his," Levison was ready to close. He picked up a club flyer from his desk. Mustafa peeped the flyer earlier- he always noticed when something was out of place.

"According to this handbill, he is in concert at the end of the month," Levison was careful with his words, "Might be lucrative for us if you... obtain him as a client."

Mustafa took a pause before reaching for the flyer. He examined it as if there was a secret compartment to the piece of card stock paper... like he was searching for a greater message than *ladies free before 11.*

"Which is about how long it will take me to find a buyer for," Levison waved at the jewels, "all of this."

Mustafa rose out of his seat, "Aight... we'll be in touch."

Mustafa glanced at Saif and the two exited the office. Saif kept his eyes on Levison all the way out the door. And, even though, Levison returned the glare, Saif knew behind the look of superiority he saw genuine fear.

Levison wanted to snarl at Saif. He believed Saif could physically pulverize his small frame. But he was also sure the repercussions of Saif's attack would be enormous. The protection of justice gave Levison an edge. But he was smart enough to leave it at a wink. And picked up the phone for another negotiation.

Mustafa and Saif shared no words on their way out of the office building. They digested the meeting in their own thoughts. Halfway across the parking garage Mustafa was the first to speak, "So, holla at Ness... Let's make sure we travelin' pass da metal detectors for dis one."

It was always business first with Mustafa

"Bet... But just so ya know," for Saif business was personal, "I'm ready to slice dat khafir's head off."

"Yeah," Mustafa understood Saif's position. "Well, right now Levison serves a purpose... Due time, akh."

CHAPTER SIX

Jummah was every Friday. The weekly worship replaced the afternoon prayer. Muslims everywhere stopped their activities to join in communal worship. For Muslim men it was obligatory.

Mustafa fulfilled that obligation at Al-Ruh his entire life. Most of Mustafa's early memories began with his life around the masjid, and nothing much had changed from his childhood. The size of the congregation didn't fluctuate. Most people who made Al-Ruh their home did so because it was where they belonged.

The congregation had a reputation for being radical or more traditional- depending on who was describing them. They relied on the Sunnah of Prophet Muhammad. They mimicked his ways and practices through the study of hadith. The women- and most of the men- dressed in customary Islamic hijab. And governed themselves more by Islamic law than the law of the land.

For Mustafa Al-Ruh was a place of familiarity except for the new face that stood at the podium. The past week had been full of change, but the new Imam leading Jummah was Mustafa's biggest eye opener to Imam Yusuf's absence. The change was distracting.

"Allah, Subannawatallah, tells us that. And, surely, Allah is most merciful," Imam Farooq continued as Mustafa checked back in, "He didn't say it would be easy. But he says he will not put anything on us that we don't have the strength to bare. You see. He is saying... Our Lord is telling you, Brothers and Sisters, that there is nothing on God's Green Earth... Not a single situation that we can encounter in Allah's magnificent creation that we don't have the strength... the muscle... the mental ability or emotional resilience or spiritual fortitude to handle. Allah tells us this in Quran. And surely the Quran is clear and without doubt."

"Takbir," a voice in the crowd spoke out.

"Allah-hu-Akbar," quite a few voices answered the statement.

"Takbir," the voice cried out again.

"Allah-hu-Akbar," once again the people answered.

Imam Farooq paused, gathered his thoughts, and waited for the people to settle. He was a smaller man than Imam Yusuf. Less charismatic in his speech... Mustafa wondered if he had what it took to lead the congregation.

"Now a hardship has been placed on our community. These... um," Imam Farooq cracked a mischievous smile, "now, I don't want anybody to get nervous... You know when those of us who came through The Nation make certain references people tend get nervous..."

The acting Imam paused for the congregation's laugh track. And then continued, "But we must understand, Dear Brothers and Sisters, that there are such things as devils... Or disbelievers who want you and the rest of the world to believe that our beloved Imam was some merciless killer instead of a leader who fought to preserve and grow his community. And it is up to us as an Ummah... as a community...

to bare this burden together. To be able to trust that we have one common goal..."

As the congregation rallied behind their temporary leader, something in Imam Farooq's statement drew Mustafa's attention to Reek. He wanted to contemplate Reek's connection to the spiritual leaders statement, but then he heard Imam Farooq say, "... to not drop our arms. To pick up the fight and maintain what Allah has prescribed for us."

And suddenly, Mustafa remembered a problem he had not handled.

"Dua," The Imam commanded. And the entire congregation dropped their heads toward cupped hands. In flawless Arabic The Imam pleaded, "Our Lord! Bestow on us endurance and make our foothold sure and give us help against those that reject faith."

The congregation bellowed out, "Ameen!"

Mustafa knew exactly what he had to do. He used the prayer to organize his thoughts. He begged Allah to purify his actions and accept his intentions. His obligation was bigger than business... he needed to protect his community. By the time Mustafa made dhikr and offered his final dua he was sure of his path.

Mustafa exited the masjid. He peeped Saif talking to Reek and Shim on the outskirts of the crowd. Mustafa could tell by the tension in Saif's shoulders they were in sync. Mustafa made his way to his pack- engaging no one. There wasn't time for small talk.

"So, what da move," Saif questioned.

"You heard Imam Farooq," Mustafa didn't have to spell it out,

"Jus' cause dey locked up da Imam don't mean we stop doin' da work. We done let him parlay long enough. Time to protect what's ours."

Shim nodded in agreement- his adrenaline pumped. As usual, Reek wasn't paying attention. The group of women moving in their direction distracted him. The most beautiful amongst them, Ayesha, stared at Mustafa.

"As-Salaammu-Alaikum, Mustafa," Ayesha sang out.

"Wa-Alaikum-Salaam, Ayesha," Mustafa glanced in her direction and then looked away.

Ayesha continued to gawk at Mustafa. Mustafa focused on his thought. Ayesha moved past him, but turned back to see if Mustafa was, at least, watching her hips sway beneath her hijab. Mustafa wasn't looking. But Reek was. And that made Ayesha turn away.

"Damn she choosing," Reek grabbed his genitals.

"Let's meet up after Isha," Mustafa ignored Reek's inappropriateness, "Should be b'iness as usual."

"If dat," Reek corrected Mustafa, "Dese khafirs sloppy, akh."

"Well, dere it is."

There was nothing left to say.

CHAPTER SEVEN

Ayanna could see from the street that all the curtains were drawn. Ordinarily, closed curtains were not something to cause someone worries. People kept their curtains closed all the time. But for Ayanna's Momma normal was never the case.

Ayanna braced herself. She knocked on the door and waited a moment before she knocked again. Ayanna wanted to give Momma a second to get herself together. But the moment seemed like it took forever. So, she fished her keys out her purse. And knocked as she unlocked the door.

The living room was dark.

"Momma," Ayanna called out.

Ayanna closed the door behind her and crept into the darkness.

"Momma?"

Ayanna suppressed her growing anxiety. She looked to the back of the house. The darkness closed in on her. Ayanna frantically searched for the light switch.

"And which one are you?"

The voice almost made Ayanna jump out of her skin. It wasn't until she gathered herself that she realized it was her mother sitting in the corner. Her dark skin was invisible in the shadows. The ash from her cigarette dimmed the light of the cherry.

"Lawd, Momma, you scared me."

"Oh, you the good one," Momma stated… as if there was a bad one.

Ayanna- relieved that the worse she discovered was her mother sitting in the dark- walked over and kissed Momma on the forehead.

"Dem people been coming by here all day."

"What people, Momma?"

"You know 'em… Tell 'em they can stop… or I'm gonna stop 'em."

Ayanna didn't want to figure out what any of it meant. She had struggled with her mother's schizophrenia her whole life. And found that sometimes the best solution was to act as if there wasn't a problem to ignore.

"Momma, why you are sitting here in the dark?"

"Dey want to see me," Momma replied to the silly question.

Ayanna tried to imagine who *they* were. She walked over to the drapes and slung them open. "Well… Let me see you. How about that?"

Beams of sunlight overtook the darkness and exposed the interior. Even in her mental state, Momma kept a clean house. The light streaked across Momma's face, and she tried to cover her eyes.

But Ayanna saw the exhaustion. Her mother hadn't slept, and Ayanna knew she needed to check Momma's medicine.

"You ain't gonna let 'em get me are you?" Momma's question was child-like. Ayanna stared out the window. She heard the need for protection. Ayanna complied with her role as guardian. But she longed for the security to be reciprocated.

"No ma'am. I won't." Ayanna held back her tears.

Ayanna spent the rest of the evening in her mother's proximity. They didn't share the space. Both lost in their own worlds. And even though their interaction was miniscule, Ayanna felt drained as she traveled on public transportation to the other side of town.

She didn't want to think about what she didn't have… or why she was chosen to deal with the lack that most people took for granted. She watched the city pass her by and used her breathing techniques to keep her mind clear of any thoughts that attempted to haunt her.

The bus came to a stop and a toddler hobbled down the aisle. A cute lil' yellow gal with multiple pigtails- pulled tight and adorned with an array of bright ribbons and beads. The lil' yellow gal's mother paid her fare and kept her eye on the fast moving toddler. The lil' yellow gal waved at all of the passengers. They responded to her cuteness.

Her mother caught up and lifted her to the seat in front of Ayanna. The lil' yellow gal couldn't sit still. But it wasn't the obnoxious-*get on my nerves*-type of restlessness. She was adorable and inquisitive… Full of energy.

Ayanna wondered, for a moment, what shaped our perspective. She thought about Black boys and fat nappy-headed Black babies. Appearance, alone, could change how, even, a baby is received. Ayanna's thoughts sometimes felt too complicated.

Eventually, the lil' yellow gal, in her exploration, turned toward

Ayanna. She stared at Ayanna for a minute. Ayanna smiled at the little ball of light.

"Aye," the child said with a smile and a wave.

The mother was checking facebook/twitter/instagram.

"Aye," the lil' yellow gal screamed out again. It was one of the few words in her arsenal. And she repeated it in rapid fire.

"Hey." Ayanna felt freed from her slump.

The sound of a strange voice speaking to her child snatched the young mother from the electronic leash, and she turned to face the speaker. Ayanna smiled.

"Sorry."

"Naw… she's good." Ayanna really wanted to say, *tonight she saved my life*. But instead she added, "She's so pretty."

"Thank you." The young mother turned to observe her daughter's beauty, and she gave her first-born a huge kiss. The toddler bubbled with joy. She showered her mother with wet open mouth kisses- mixed with laughter. They had played the game before. And as the young mother teasingly wiped her daughters saliva from her cheeks, Ayanna was slammed back into her unhappiness.

Ayanna tried to hold onto her smile as long as she could. And when the tears welled up in her eyes, she turned away from the public display of joy. Ayanna decided she was close enough to home and could walk the rest of the way. Ayanna exited without speaking- quietly wondering if the lil' yellow gal would notice.

The end of summer breeze was perfect for a walk. Emotionally Ayanna was too far-gone to enjoy it. She was ready to shut the world out. Ayanna raced up the stairs of her apartment. Once inside, she peeled the layers off, leaving a trail of clothes behind her... even though she carried years of disappointment on her back. Ayanna turned on the shower; the scalding water couldn't completely drown her dis/ease. But it was a start.

Ayanna slipped on her cotton jogging pants and a wife beater. She opened a bottle of red wine, and retrieved a wooden cigar box from the cabinet above the refrigerator. In the middle of her ritual her phone made a noise...

It is a text is from Yasmeen: YOU NEED TO GET YOUR ASS OUT THE HOUSE FOR SOMETHING OTHER THAN A RALLY #TURNUP

Ayanna shook her head and respond: JUST CAME FROM MOMMA... NOT TONIGHT

Ayanna knew Yasmeen would not push back once she read that.

Yasmeen: U GOOD?

Ayanna: BOUT TO B... HIT U 2MORROW.

Ayanna tossed her phone to the side and resumed her ritual. She rolled a perfect joint... a skill she had learned *along the way*. She drug into the living room and flopped down on the couch. Ayanna grabbed the remote, and Meshell NdegeoCello blared from the speakers.

Ayanna lit an incense... frankincense and mur *to drive out the spirits*. She took her time to burn an even cherry at the tip of her joint. The first puff traveled straight to her gut. She held the smoke. Not sure if it was the THC or the lack of oxygen, but Ayanna felt light.

She took a big gulp of her wine and escaped into her own world.

CHAPTER EIGHT

Reek glided into the driveway and dismounted his high performance BMX with one clean swoop. After he secured it on its kickstand, Reek walked over to the Monte Carlo, in the driveway. He circled his automobile. It was a 1988 SS, black with red racing stripes on the trunk. He peeped into the window. The seats were black leather with red piping. Reek caressed the car. He loved the spoils of war.

Reek darted onto the front porch. He adjusted his mask. Reek was a chameleon... authentic to his environment. His true self was so deeply hidden; he had no clue how to identify it.

It was time for him to play father and husband.

The inside of the two-bedroom bungalow was *unkept*... not filthy, but not clean either. There were dirty dishes in the sink. Overflowing trash in the kitchen. A pile of clothes on the couch. Clutter on the coffee table. And in front of the flat screen television 6-year-old Rashad sat on the floor, surrounded by his toys; hypnotized by his greatest influence.

The man walking through the front door didn't pull Rashad's attention from the television, at first. Rashad turned, and the two tried to place the other. It took a moment before either spoke. Reek, the father, nodded his head. Rashad, the son, waved at his pops. Reek looked around the house like he was searching for someone else.

"Where's ya Momma at?" Reek whispered.

Rashad pointed to the back.

"Okay." Reek wondered how long had his son been alone. But he was, also, relieved he still had time before he had to deal with the boy's mother.

"Well, how ya doin'?" Reek stretched out his arms, "Come give your Abu a hug."

Rashad was hesitant, but Reek urged him on- motioned with his hands for Rashad to come over. And reluctantly, Rashad pulled himself from his high-definition babysitter and trudged toward his father.

Reek blamed Rashad's mother for his son's timid personality... His selective memory never accounted for his absence. As soon as the boy got within arms distance, Reek yanked Rashad into his chest. The jerking movement made the boy tense up- at first- but as his father stabbed him with tickles the child loosened up.

"Slaama-Laikum... Slaama-Laikum. You miss your Abu, huh?"

The rhetorical question was followed by tickles.

"I miss ya too... Wallahee. I miss my lil' man."

Rashad giggled and Reek felt less like a stranger. His father freed him and the happy little boy rushed over to his spot in front of the idiot box. He grabbed his newest toy and brought the toy back to Reek. It was his way of including his father in his life.

"What ya got dere?" Reek conjured interest.

The bedroom door creaked open before Rashad could answer.

And Rashida Henry, Reek's second wife, stormed out the room. His first wife, Naeemah, was a more demure young lady, who lived across the country with her parents and Reek's daughter. The first wife was born Muslim, and her father came and rescued her from Reek's antics.

But Rashida converted to Islam through Reek's teachings. Her birth name was Sharekiah, but her stage name was Poison. Reek *rescued* her from the strip club and taught her his understanding of Islam.

Sharekiah, tired of being run through by countless men and women, gravitated towards the doctrine that protected the softer sex. And Reek sold her on his façade. He convinced her she did not have to worry about providing for herself because that was his job. On top of his religious beliefs, Reek was a street nigga. The contradiction intrigued Sharekiah.

"Shad, I thought I told you I was taking a…" Rashida stopped in her steps when she saw Reek. "Oh… It's you… Is it my night already?"

Reek ignored her sarcasm, "Slaama-Laikum."

Rashida didn't respond.

"Slaama-Laikum," Reek repeated himself. This time he loaded the greeting of peace with a warning.

Rashida rolled her eyes, "Laikum-Salaam."

Reek's anger welled up, but Rashad tugged at his shirt… he had not finished showing his father his toy. Reek seemingly redirected his attention to his son. He picked Rashad up into his arms… the little

51

boy was a prop.

"Ask your Ummi instead of all dat attitude, how about what she gonna fix Abu for dinner?" Reek thought his son wouldn't understand the laden statement if he followed it with a tickle and a kiss.

Rashida understood. But she was tired of not having the dream Reek promised her. Rashida had provided for herself better when she was swinging on a pole. She couldn't contain her frustration and pulled empty cabinets open and slammed them shut. After she made her way around the kitchen she discovered a box of Hamburger Helper and banged it onto the counter.

"Tell your Abu I would love to cook somethin', and- maybe- if he would stop followin' behind Uncle Mustafa and actually put some steaks in da freezer, I'd have somethin' to cook."

Reek didn't like being challenged by a woman. The box to his kill switch raised, and he glared at Rashida- exposing the souls he carried in his eyes. She tried to return his gaze, but looked away. Rashida knew there were no more buttons to push before their confrontation went too far.

Reek eyes stayed fixated on Rashida as he set Rashad down.

"Rashad go watch some TV while Abu talks to your Ummi alone."

The little boy looked up at his father, but Reek didn't break his stare. Rashad wondered what had gone aerie. He sensed the tension; felt the energy change. And with no comfort from his father, Rashad turned to his mother for answers.

Despite her shortcomings, Rashida loved her son and wanted to protect him. She feigned a smile. And nodded her head for Rashad to follow his fathers instructions. Rashad wasn't old enough to stay and defend his mother from harm. But he didn't want to leave her either.

"Go ahead baby... I'm okay," she lied.

Rashad gave his father one more look, even though Reek didn't notice. Then after a moment, Rashad walked back to his spot in front of the tube. Rashida watched him and once he sat down, she turned back toward Reek.

Reek bolted toward her, grabbed her arm, and pulled her toward the bedroom. Rashida tried to pull her arm back but lacked the strength. Reek used Rashida as door opener. And once he pushed her through, he slammed the door behind him.

Rashad stared at the door. And listened to the screams and banging that resonated from the room. The television could no longer hold his attention. Rashad would remember the yelling like it went on forever. And by the time the screams of violence transformed into moans of passion, Rashad had fallen asleep.

Reek and Rashida's relationship was to fight and fuck. It was how they defined love, and their individual backgrounds fueled the dysfunction. Rashida was from an abusive upbringing, the classic stripper cliché... Her body developed early. The men, who were supposed to protect her, were the ones who took advantage of her.

So, she chose Reek. *Her soul mate.* Shuffled through foster families and group homes. He had no foundation for healthy love, either. The fact the two dealt with one another despite their toxic interaction was symbolic of their insanity.

As Rashida lay stark naked beneath the covers, she watched Reek lace up his combat boots. Now that the fucking was over she was ready to return to the fight.

"Where you going? I thought it was my night."

"I got some bi'ness to handle."

"Nigga dis ain't what I signed up for..."

Reek was always ready for battle. He stopped lacing up his boots and stared over his shoulder.

Rashida realized she didn't want to go another round. And wondered if *going to handle some business* meant money was on the horizon. She didn't want to destroy her chances at receiving a piece of the pie. Rashida was the primary caretaker of their son, but that didn't guarantee Reek would bring home the halal bacon. His every move was contingent on what he felt from moment to moment.

"I 'on't mean no disrespect." She removed the covers from her flesh and crawled behind her husband. Rashida pressed her perfectly sculpted body against Reek's back and wrapped her arms around his shoulder. Rashida had mastered the art of finesse.

"I am just saying that I agreed to be your second wife because I thought you were a king," she whispered in his ear and kissed his neck, "I understand that a good leader gotta be able to follow."

Another kiss. She grinded her hips, on his back, so he felt the moisture between her thighs...

"You taught me that, my husband. But as your wife ain't it my duty to tell you when you slippin'."

Rashida made her way to Reek's other ear and whispered, "You shouldn't be Mustafa's foot soldier... You greater dan dat. Stop lettin' him play you."

Rashida's words consumed Reek. He agreed with his concubine. He didn't plan on being in Mustafa's shadow for long. But Reek was cunning in his own rite, and he wasn't going to let anybody, including Rashida, play him. He stood up and unhinged himself from Rashida's grasp.

"Just be patient. I got my own plans. Right now- I got some bi'ness to handle."

Rashida stared at him. She didn't believe he had a plan. And it pissed her off that Reek pulled away from her web.

"Well, I hope whatever 'bi'ness' you handle brings some money in dis house… cause dis shit gettin' old."

Reek grabbed his pistol from the dresser. And put one in the chamber. The sound of the metal made Rashida jump.

"Yeah it is." Reek stared at Rashida to punctuate his actions. And then walked to the door. "Slaama-Laikum."

Rashida didn't respond.

Reek turned toward her. This time he wouldn't repeat himself.

Rashida rolled her eyes. "Laikum-Salaam."

CHAPTER NINE

Keisha's cough turned into convulsions. Every muscle in her upper torso retracted over and over again. It sounded like, if her spell continued, she would cough up a lung.

Rico looked up and smirked.

Rico took pleasure in other peoples pain... their weaknesses amused him. It made selling dope an easy profession. There were no late nights of guilt or paranoia from wrongdoings. Rico's conscious was void. And he wore the lack of regard on his sleeve.

He looked tailor-made for the life. The constant *beefs* scarred Rico's brown skin. His light brown eyes looked evil and ghost-like. His muscular frame seemed like he had sculpted it in the penitentiary... although he never acknowledged doing any time.

In Rico's mind, Keisha wasn't strong enough for his world. It didn't matter how raw she presented herself. She was a woman... and for Rico, *cain't no bitch run shit*. Rico kept her around because Keisha *had a phat ass*... dark, flawless skin, ample breasts, and a small waist. She even had a pretty smile when she used it.

Rico felt like if he constant presence meant, eventually, he would *smash*. Like most super predators, Rico could wait for the kill. Plus, Rico loved to see Keisha *pull a nigga's hoe card*. She was known for spitting on niggas, pistol-whipping grown-ass men, and stealing hoes from other pimps. And at the end of the day, Rico trusted that Keisha saw all the angles; so for him it was smarter to have Keisha on his team.

Keisha's coughing fit made Smoke and June look up from their monotonous routine of bagging up dope...

"Damn... Keisha cain't handle dat Keisha, huh?" The big grin widened June's huge face. He was a gorilla. An enormous guy, who threw around his weight. A loud country boy, and, like most country boys, June's thirst for violence involved hand-to-hand combat.

June didn't have the propensity for killing that infected the inner city. This made him weak to Keisha, who grew up in Fourth Ward- a neighborhood known for its incurable *pistol-play*.

"Shut your fat ass up, nigga!" And to punctuate her point Keisha hit the blunt, which had the adverse effect she was hoping for... Keisha's coughing ensued, again. This time it made her eyes bulge out of their sockets.

"Give me my dope, bruh!" Rico jumped up and grabbed his blunt- with no debate from Keisha.

"Damn Rico. What ya got over dere?" Smoke jabbed.

Rico and Smoke shared a quick glance, and the two grinned. They were both on the prowl.

Smoke- his skin colored blue-black- was a hardened killer. He grew up in Adamsville. And had been running with Rico, ever since Rico appeared in Allen Temple or The Temp, as locals called it. The infamous apartment complex was Adamsville's Holy Mecca, where everybody rotated around the rock... and they yearned to kiss the stone.

Like Rico, Smoke's humor was sinister. But Keisha didn't mouth off to Smoke like she did to June. The legend had it that Smoke shot his girlfriend in the face for raising her voice. Nobody ever debated the tale.

Keisha cleared her throat, "Whew shit. What da hell? Y'all niggas be getting too high for me."

Keisha needed to get out of their sights. She realized she was always being hunted. She couldn't show a kink in her armor. Keisha grabbed her purse and coughed all the way to the bathroom.

Rico, June, and Smoke watched her leave. Looking at her butt like it was the first time they had seen one. They were thankful it was still a few weeks of summer left. So, Keisha could continue her parade of cut-off shorts and spandex pants with spaghetti- strap tops. Nobody said a word until Keisha closed the bathroom door.

"Dem throat muscles ain't gettin' 'nough exercise," Rico stated.

June burst out laughing.

"Hell naw," Smoke agreed.

Inside the bathroom, Keisha dropped her hard demeanor and placed her hand on her chest. Keisha waved her face to down. She felt anxious. She turned on the faucet and sucked water from the faucet. She looked in the mirror, and slowed down her breathing.

"God damn," she said to herself.

After Keisha settled, she opened her purse, took out the pearl handled chrome 380, set it on the counter, and fished around in her purse until she found a tampon. She peeled off the tight shorts and thongs, sat on the toilet, and became a woman again.

Back in the living room, Keisha was still the topic of conversation.

"Nigga, I 'on't see shit but dat phat ass... I don't care what team she swangin' for," Rico proclaimed.

"Just gotta wait it out," Smoke co-signed.

Rico poked out his chest, grabbed his imaginary lapel, and nodded. It was his way of saying he was the king of waiting it out... *Presidential and political with his game.* Everybody in the room comprehended the nonverbal communication. And as if the trumpets sounded in Rico's honor, car lights flashed through the blinds and the music from outside filled up the room.

"Bout time dat nigga get here wit' da food." June didn't have the game to get Keisha, and he couldn't fantasize about sex on an empty stomach.

Rico snickered, "Look at you wit' ya face. Always worryin' 'bout some food. Betta make sure ya greedy ass watchin' dat scale... Both dem moafuckas."

Rico peeped out the window... Rico unlocked the door and turned his attention back to June.

Outside, Kenny, a scrawny little guy, had pulled into the driveway and sat in the car- rapping along to the music. He was live in concert. Kenny was a do-boy and things like gangsta rap music is where he got his swag.

Even though Kenny served as a pincushion. In Kenny's mind it wouldn't be long before him and Rico hit it big. And then he would have naked women to supervise... historians would one day refer to Kenny's aspirations as *The Nino Brown Effect*.

As the song came to an end, Kenny opened the car door. His eyes closed tight- spitting with all his heart. He was *Lil' Young Sleazy Gangsta Thug*. He cut off the ignition, and brought his concert to an end...

But instead of applause, the double barrel of a sawed-off shotgun stared him in the face.

Kenny's eyes widened. He strained to see past the two holes of the barrel- both dark and hollow. On the other end of the gun was a ghost, dressed in all black- with a black and white scarf draped around its head. The figure spoke no words.

Inside, Rico continued to run his mouth...

"I'm sayin' look at dis nigga... You think he needs more food?"

Smoke sneered at the comment. June's embarrassment was entertaining. Even though, June's country ass could beat Rico's head in; Rico's city-slick bravado had June fooled.

Kenny opened the door slowly.

Rico peeped over his shoulder and then looked at June, "Dere it is! Delivery or Dijourno nigga... Don't matter do it?"

Smoke chuckled.

Nobody noticed Kenny frozen and spooked in the doorway.

Rico finally turned around "Nigga, hell is you waitin' on... close da door."

Just as Rico finished his last word, the butt of a shotgun hit Kenny in the back of his head. He fell to the floor- sending hot wings, with lemon pepper sprinkles, everywhere. On queue, four masked figures bum-rushed the house. Before Rico, Smoke, or June knew what had hit them, each of them had a chopper pointed to their dome.

The gunman in front of Rico cocked his double barrel and spoke through his keffiyeh, "Tell your boys to simmer down, now."

In the bathroom, Keisha heard the ruckus and crept to the door. She heard the sound of metal clicking. Her heart pounded. She knew what was happening on the other side...

"Fuck you nigga!"

"Ya said dat already when ya set up shop," Mustafa said as he pulled the scarf from around his face. "Ain't no need to repeat ya'self, playboy."

"Hell you lookin' at," Reek sounded off from the table.

Mustafa heard Reek's voice and caught a glimpse of him out of his peripheral. Reek was jumpy and Smoke looked like he was going to snap. Reek burrowed his muzzle into Smoke's temple

"Lower ya gaze, bitch ass nigga!"

Smoke's breathes got heavier.

Reek egged him on, "Do somethin'!"

Mustafa tried to ignore the distraction and remain locked in on Rico. But he could sense the tipping point.

"Ya good, akh?"

Rico eyed his gun on the couch. His action didn't go unnoticed. Mustafa tightened his grip on the shotgun.

"I'll chop dis devils head off, akh!" Reek was a time bomb.

"Chill, akh," Saif stepped in.

Mustafa knew he had to get them out of there, "Look, my guys is gettin' restless. Bottom line- ain't no workin' over here. I know ya know dat already."

"Nigga ya need to keep up wit' da news," Rico sneered, "Y'all done over here."

The statement bothered Mustafa. He knew the Imam's arrest would make their enemies think they were weak as an Ummah. He had to hold the line.

"Da only niggas done ova here is y'all," Mustafa nodded to Shim, "So, my man is gonna take ya do-boy and round up da dope and da money... Just look at it as charity to da community."

Shim grabbed Kenny by his collar. Kenny tried to break free, which looked more like a slapstick comedy routine.

"Kenny, you betta not give 'em shit!" Rico disregarded Mustafa's demand.

And Mustafa responded by smacking Rico in the mouth with his tool. Rico's lips exploded with blood. He let out a loud grunt, before he took a knee. He swayed back and forth for a moment... Mustafa kicked him in the mouth to finish the job. With Rico flat on his back, Mustafa straddled him and shoved the steel right into Rico's mouth. Rico choked on the barrel and his cracked teeth.

Mustafa spoke in an eerie calm, "Now, Kenny, we 'on't want no problems, but we gotta tax y'all for disrespectin' da Ummah. You see, Rico here thinks it's okay to shit in my yard and tell me 'fuck me' while he's doin' it," Mustafa paused and pushed the barrel deeper into Rico's throat, "And the only reason I haven't blown a hole through his forehead is because like My Lord I am merciful... But like My Lord dat mercy has its limits."

Mustafa pulled the shotgun out of Rico's mouth and popped him again. Rico seemed to lie out cold.

Mustafa turned the shotgun to Kenny.

"Get da fuckin' dope Kenny!"

Shim slung Kenny across the room. Kenny jumped up and scrambled toward the cabinet where the dope was stashed.

Suddenly, the bathroom door flew open...

Keisha burst out the door...

She shot wildly... sending the room into a frenzy.

Kenny tried to duck for cover, but he was the first one hit.

Shim whirled to the bathroom to open fire, but got hit twice... once in the shoulder and the other in the chest.

Mustafa turned and raised his stick, but before he could let off a shot, Rico pulled a switchblade and stabbed him in his leg.

Saif didn't hesitate... he shot June in the head and then popped Keisha.

Smoke made his move. He used his forearm to force Reek's gun upwards and Reek shot into the ceiling. The blast threw Reek off balance, and Smoke scrambled to the kitchen. Reek tried to recover and bust Smoke from behind, but his aim was off... and all he took out was a chunk of the doorway.

Rico dashed for his heat. And as Mustafa pulled the knife from his leg, Rico let off two shots- while he back peddled to the door. He only hit sheetrock.

Mustafa ducked, took aim, and hit Rico in the shoulder. The force from the shot sent Rico tumbling out the door; Rico finished his roll, sprung to his feet, and took off into the night.

Before Mustafa could try and wobble after him, automatic gunfire rang out into the living room. Smoke's reappearance into the kitchen doorway sent everybody clambering for their lives. Smoke had the biggest gun, and the odds had flipped to his favor.

"Fuck y'all think this is?" Smoke let off more rounds in Reek's direction… behind the upturned table.

"Think you can tell me where to set up shop?" He shot in Saif's vicinity… behind a lazy boy

"Flatlands, nigga!" Smoke saw the top of Mustafa's head… behind the couch. He edged in closer.

Smoke crept toward the couch. His eyes darted between Saif and Reek's hiding spots. He hoped they wanted play jack-in-the-box.

Mustafa, Saif, and Reek tried to figure out their next move. The cover was a joke. Smoke had bought the classic AK-47 to the party and there was no way their current hiding spaces would suffice. It was a matter of time before Smoke picked them off- one by one.

Mustafa felt Smoke was dangerously close. But he was trapped. In his mind, he made supplication… a prayer for his soul.

Smoke was on top of him. He sneered. And raised his weapon for the kill shot.

A single round was fired.

But Mustafa didn't feel the burn of hot metal traveling through his skull.

Mustafa looked up at Smoke. Smoke's eyes widened. And then he flopped down on the sofa… exhausted. Only the hole at the base of his head meant he would not wake up from his nap.

Mustafa eased up from his hiding space and saw Shim on the ground with the smoking gun in his hand. Saif and Reek crept from their hideouts.

Mustafa staggered to his feet.

Saif ran over to Mustafa. "You aight?"

Mustafa waved Saif off, "Go get Shim."

Saif, quickly changed directions and went to lift Shim's big bloody body from the floor. His injury was mild compared to the hole in Shim's chest. Shim was leaking at a dangerous rate.

Mustafa looked at the death that surrounded him. He knew his crew was lucky to be walking out alive. And the four remaining dead bodies wouldn't just disappear.

As Mustafa turned to leave out of the door, he saw Reek run toward the cabinet…

"What you doing?"

The question was ridiculous, but Reek answered anyway, "Gettin' dis fuckin' work, akh!"

Mustafa watched Saif drag Shim off the battlefield.

"We gotta go!" Mustafa knew they needed to get the work. But the sirens in the distance meant the real trouble was on its way. Mustafa limped as fast as he could to the door.

Reek watched Mustafa leave and finished grabbing everything he could get his hands on. He was happy to collect the booty on his own. And once he gathered the spoils, he ran to Mustafa's side, and helped him into the van.

Moments later, the van- stolen for the job- swerved onto Dill Ave. Shim laid in the back- his heart pumped blood out of his body. Once the adrenaline subsided, the pain heightened. Shim tried to muffle his scream. Saif gripped Shim's hand. And the grip crushed Saif's bones.

"Hol' on... jus' hol' on Shim," Saif ignored his pain for the pain of his brother, "stay wit' me bruh!"

Mustafa tried to center his thoughts. He needed to figure out his next five steps, in the midst of all the confusion. Mustafa took the scarf from around his neck and tied the scarf as tight as he could to stop the bleeding.

Reek took another wild turn.

"Slow it down, akh." Mustafa ordered.

Reek checked his mirrors and tried to calm himself.

"Put pressure on dem holes," Mustafa's clarity kicked in.

Saif followed the commands and took the scarf from around his neck to stop the bleeding.

"Head to da warehouse offa Murphy," Mustafa said to Reek as he pulled a cellphone out of the glove compartment. "Lemme see if I can get Black to meet us over dere."

CHAPTER TEN

The phone rang for the fourth time before Ayanna moved around in her sleep. She had passed out on the couch. The afternoon she spent with her mother. Her feelings of loneliness. The little girl on the bus she wanted to be… or wanted for herself. It all took a toll on Ayanna. A bottle of wine and a joint of OG Kush erased her problems.

By the fifth ring, she sat up. But even as she clawed for the phone, part of her remained in slumber.

"Hello… yeah, I'm up," she lied, "What's up?"

Brittany was on the other side of the line. Her tone was frantic. Ayanna couldn't catch every word… There was a problem… something about her mother's house on fire… they were at the hospital…

"What? I was just over there… when did that happen? She all right? So, where y'all at right now? I don't have a ride… Well, why didn't you come and get me? No, I am not saying it's your responsibility. I'm just saying if you cannot handle it… No, Britt… hold on… Brittany, I am not about to get into this with you… Okay, okay! Let me see what I can do."

Ayanna hung up the phone and dropped her head into her hands.

"Fuck me!" She screamed out to whoever was listening. She was alone.

Ayanna didn't understand what happened. She submitted to the ebb and flow of life- its peaks and valleys- but sometimes it felt as if she lived her life in the low country.

She reached for the half of joint in her ashtray. Weed had long left its recreational position in Ayanna's life. Cannabis was medicinal, and the deep drag allowed her to put everything in its proper compartments.

On the other side of town, a lemon colored mini-dress hugged Yasmeen's curves as she sat at the bar. Her ebony skin glowed with a bronze undertone. She shimmered it with gold flecks. Her full dark lips- glossed. Her naturally long lashes- brushed. She wore just the right amount of jewelry and carried the perfect hand purse.

Two guys dressed in the unoriginal *jeans/ suit jacket/ button down shirt/ slick bottom/ shoes uniform* stood in front of her. They were hyperactive puppies trying to impress their master for a treat. Yasmeen marveled at their lack of authenticity. But for Yasmeen relationships served a material purpose, or they had no place in her life. She used the two squares for a free shot of chilled patron.

The lamer of the two coughed as he downed the shot. Yasmeen was even more turned off. Yasmeen's high tolerance for alcohol often worked in her favor; kept her from being in compromising positions due to a loss of control. But it was a hindrance, at the moment, because she would need at least one more shot before she cut them loose.

"You might want to put a helmet on your lil' partna right there." Yasmeen loved to *son a nigga*. "Because if that's too strong for you- imagine what will happen if you have to swallow me?"

The rousing statement had nothing to do with the lapdog's chances of exploring her amazing body. Yasmeen was provocative by nature. She shared no physical attraction to the lad. Although, Yasmeen's pursuit of the finer things could measure attraction wallet-deep. When her phone rang, Yasmeen was relieved.

"I tell you what... Why don't you go let your chest cool down and if I haven't found something else to get into, you can come back and buy another round." Yasmeen continued her flirtatious emasculation with a pinch on the lil' boy's cheek. Sadly, Yasmeen thought, they'd be back. She twirled around in her chair, and they stood there- neither having a clue how far they should stray.

"Girl, please tell me you've changed your mind about coming out... These lame niggas is killing me."

Ayanna didn't give Yasmeen the response she had hoped. There was urgency in her friend's voice. Ayanna was one of a select few, whose friendship didn't come with conditions.

"What happened? When?" Yasmeen gathered her things as she collected the rest of the info, "Okay... Yani, I'm on my way."

It took Yasmeen less than forty-five minutes to leave Buckhead, pick up Ayanna from Cabbagetown, and make it to The Atlanta Medical Center on Boulevard. Yasmeen paid good money for her platinum BMW 645Li, and didn't need an emergency to drive like a wild woman. But a legitimate reason to do the dash was welcomed.

In the hospital waiting room, Ayanna's sister, Brittany waited impatiently for her sister. Her long weave and straight back gave Brittany's appearance haughtiness. And even though Brittany came from meager means, she felt she had worked hard enough to not be surrounded by lower class germs.

Brittany's husband, Ralph- a sweater vest/fitted-Dockers type of guy- sat next to her. He rubbed his hands over his thick Indian-like hair. Their son, Samuel, sat with his head on his mother's lap. Their perfect mulatto family looked atypical held hostage inside the inner city hospital.

The television in the waiting area played the local news.

"This just in, police are on the scene of the West End, where a shooting has taken place. We join Phaedra Jones who is live…"

"Ayanna's favorite side of town isn't it?" Ralph sarcastically commentated.

"Mmm… Heathens," Brittany responded. Her good Christian values kept her from consorting with those types of people… whoever those people were. Although, Brittany's Christ-like values, somehow, left room for general judgment.

The elevator bell caught Ralph's attention; he tapped Brittany and nodded toward Yasmeen and Ayanna as they rushed off the elevator.

Brittany rolled her eyes.

By the time Brittany regained her focus, Ayanna was standing over her, "Where's momma?"

"Glad you could make it," Brittany jabbed.

Yasmeen knew her presence added to Brittany's frustration. Yas couldn't hide her satisfaction, "Hey Britt."

Brittany gave a smug smile and nodded her head.

"Britt, what are they saying about momma?" Ayanna didn't care about her sister's disapproval.

Brittany couldn't control herself. She didn't like Yasmeen, and Brittany expressed every thought out loud. Yasmeen dressed in her *turn-up outfit*, fueled Brittany's disgust.

"I'm sorry- this is family business could you excuse us Yasmeen... Please and thank you."

"Family business?" Yasmeen fired back.

Ayanna placed her hand on Yasmeen's shoulder, "Brittany, I needed a ride. And Yasmeen's like family."

"Oh, I am sure she is someone's family, sweetie." The comment hit below the belt. But Brittany judgment caused her to loose jurisdiction over her mouth.

"Ladies, we are all under a lot of pressure. Let's..." Ralph's attempt to step in was shot down with Brittany's glare. Ralph put his hands up in surrender (a move he had learned from watching The Cosby Show). He retracted, "I'm... I'm just trying to say that I am sure we are all concerned about your mother and..."

No matter what Ralph said he would end up with his foot in his mouth. Brittany decided to save him, "Ralph... How about you be a dear and go get me some coffee... Or something... Me and my sister have family business to discuss."

The statement was final and everybody recognized.

"Sounds like a good idea," Ralph turned to Yasmeen, "How about it, Yas... Can I interest you in an industrial cup of Java?"

Yasmeen never shied away from battle, but she was there for her friend. "Yeah, that's cool." She broke her glare from Brittany and looked at Ayanna, "If you need me, Yani, I'll be right over here... Sis." She made sure to emphasize the last word.

"Thank you" Ayanna responded. Her gratitude was not for Yasmeen standing in proximity, but she was more thankful that Yasmeen didn't go from zero to a hundred.

Ralph picked up his son and headed to the coffee station with Yasmeen.

"I don't like her," Brittany blurted out without even checking to make sure Yasmeen was out of earshot.

"She hasn't done anything to you, Britt."

"She isn't proper..."

Ayanna believed the judgment was less about Yasmeen and more about Brittany's perspective on Ayanna's life. She didn't have time to analyze it, "What did the doctors say about momma?"

And as if they had been watching from the cameras, the doctor walked in. Behind the MD was a heavyset woman in a cheap business suit set.

Brittany stood and straightened her clothes.

Ayanna turned toward them and squared her shoulders. As far as Ayanna was concerned doctors were apart of the system, and the lady behind him was definitely a member of the regime.

"Ladies," the doctor nodded.

"How is my mother," Brittany's preoccupation with superficial things was replaced with genuine worry.

"Well, the good news is besides minor smoke inhalation your mother didn't sustain any major injuries, but we still want to keep her overnight just to make sure."

"Of course," Brittany always agreed with the proper authorities.

Ayanna was the opposite. She detected nonsense on the horizon. And once she read: Helen Clark- Social Worker on the woman's ID Badge, Ayanna concluded her assumptions were correct.

"And who is she?" Ayanna confronted things head on.

"Well, although, your mothers injuries were minor," the doctor explained, "There are some major concerns about her ability to care for herself."

"Who is she?" Ayanna didn't have time for double talk.

"I am from the Department of Mental Health Services," Helen was eager to state her position and exercise her power, "and because of your mothers... condition we feel like..."

Ayanna cut her short, "My mother's condition is schizophrenia, and she has been cleared by her doctors to live by herself as long as we check in on her."

Ayanna peeped where the conversation was headed.

"Well, it was her doctor who notified us ma'am… so, evidently you haven't been checking in on her enough."

"Looka here..."

Brittany realized danger was right around the corner. As acting matriarch, she shot her sister a reprimanding glare. "What my sister is trying to say is… we check on our mother regularly, but there's no way for us to account for her actions twenty four hours a day."

"No. Not what I was gonna say." The road to Ayanna loosing her temper had no roadblocks. Helen Clark- Social Worker and Ayanna- Rebel readied for a Mexican Stand-off. But Mrs. Clark- without her title- knew *she didn't want none…* and she turned back towards Brittany, who seemed like the safer choice.

"To address to your statement, ma'am… your inability to be one hundred percent accountable is exactly why I am here. What happened with your mother tonight could have resulted into something much more serious. So, The State…"

"Here it comes," Ayanna interrupted.

"So, The State," Helen repeated herself and peppered more authority into her tone, "has decided to petition the court for your mother to be remanded to twenty four hour supervision- which if it can't be provided by the family; it will be handled by us."

Everyone was speechless for a moment.

"And what does 'it will be handled by us' entail," Brittany inquired.

"Well…"

But before the social worker gave her pitch, Ayanna interjected, "It doesn't matter- we will be doing this without your help… But thanks anyway."

"Ayanna?" Brittany didn't want to be embarrassed

"What?" For Ayanna the embarrassment was conforming to the system. "We don't want nor need their help."

Helen didn't intimidate Ayanna. But the social worker had The State on her side, "Well, like I said- we will be petitioning the court, and hopefully you can prove yourselves to be fit guardians."

Ayanna was done talking to Helen Clark- Social Worker and turned back toward the doctor, "When can we see my momma?"

There was a moment of awkward silence... Not Brittany, Helen, or the doctor knew how to deal with such controlled rebellion.

"The nurses are getting her settled and will let you know when she is ready," The doctor responded.

Ayanna sized up Helen and walked off.

Brittany tried to clean up the mess, "Thank you... Thank you." She didn't quite know what she was grateful for. She just felt like she was supposed to be indebted.

By the time Brittany reached her group, Ayanna was already fuming in her seat. Yasmeen and Ralph were back from their coffee run. And they could tell from Ayanna's face that her and Britt's family business had hit a rough spot.

"Everything okay?" Yasmeen whispered

"Hell naw," Ayanna responded loud enough for everybody to hear, even though she stared directly at the TV.

"More details just in from this massive shooting in the West End..."

CHAPTER ELEVEN

Holderness St was alive with activity. The spectacle of blue lights could be seen from Ralph David Abernathy Blvd. Residents had come from every street that ran parallel and perpendicular. This was their neighborhood. They hid from the shots, but once the smoke cleared, the citizens wanted to know what happened.

At the center of the activity was Phaedra Jones, Channel 2's star field reporter. Phaedra's team of a make-up artist, a camera operator, and a producer accompanied her.

The residents looked on as their violent reality broadcasted live. The informed dwellers of the West End recognized exploitation. Their community was full of more than the summary of crime and violence transmitted on the 6 o'clock news.

"It has been confirmed that three men and one female are dead inside this West End home. Police aren't releasing any more information at this time. This is Phaedra Jones reporting live from the West End. Back to you Bill."

Phaedra waited for the 10-second time delay... the uncomfortable silence that her and the audience had to live through during her live remote.

"That's a wrap," her producer announced.

As Phaedra's team closed down their production, Phaedra saw

the black Crown Victoria pull up to the curve. She watched the superstar detective exit his vehicle.

Detective Zimmer working the case, as lead, was *a breaking story*, in and of itself. Phaedra considered a quick interview, but Zimmer's arrival also brought with it tension from the Islamic onlookers… and that made Phaedra want to get out of dodge.

Detective Zimmer realized amongst Muslims his name had made its way onto a list that included people like Salmon Rushdie or Bill O'Reilly. But he accepted his gift and curse. Zimmer believed the superhero was not always loved.

The tailored-crusader didn't shy away from eye contact as he made his way toward the crime scene. Zimmer walked pass Phaedra and her producer as they wrapped their segment. The story hungry journalist surprised Zimmer, when she didn't bombard him with her camera. Zimmer was, slightly, offended.

"Let's get out of here before they start flying planes into something."

Zimmer smirked when he heard Phaedra's words. The statement fed his ego. It was Zimmer's bravery that made him more important than the flock he guarded. He crossed the yellow tape.

Officer Smith greeted him, "Detective Zimmer?"

Zimmer extended his hand; there was no need to confirm his identity. "You first on scene?"

"That's right. Been working this neighborhood for 15 years. So when the call came in I was already familiar with the new activity here… And wasn't that surprised to be honest."

"And why's that?" Zimmer was almost afraid to ask. *The Boys in Blue* had a tendency to be close-minded and a tad bit racist. So, there was no telling what would spring from Officer Smith's tongue.

Zimmer wasn't a racist. As an officer of the law he used stereotypes and biases as methods of carrying out his duties. There was truth to: a black man in a hooded sweatshirt, walking between houses, at night, could be up to no good; it wasn't ridiculous to assume a serial killer was white… or that a white woman would lie about rape. Every stereotype possessed a social and historical context.

"The religious fanatics have a habit of terrorizing drug dealers that try and set up shop around here," Officer Smith stated plainly.

Zimmer was thankful that the statement didn't have as much bite as it could've. "There's a twist… So, we got any witnesses?"

Smith looked confused and then turned to the crowd. Zimmer followed Smith's gaze. They both digested the crowd.

"Yeah," Zimmer chuckled, "I guess we're the insurgents around here… But keep poking. And get me a list of possible terrorists that have the muscle to pull this off."

"I'm on it Detective."

Zimmer walked up on the porch. Every officer, no matter how engaged in securing the scene, took the time to acknowledge Zimmer; happy to be traveling with the megastar.

Zimmer paused in the threshold. Great detective work took single-mindedness, and Zimmer needed to shut out all the glitz and accolades. He moved pass the part of his ego that couldn't differentiate between the forensic photographers and the paparazzi.

Zimmer silenced the chatter in his head. He took note of everything… From the bullet placards to the arrangement of the furniture… no detail was too small. He looked at the sheets that covered the dead bodies. Bleeding ghost on oak floors.

Thomas walked over, two junior detectives trailed behind him. He was glad it was Zimmer's turn to work lead. There was no secret to the difficulties involved with cracking a case in the West End.

"Glad you could grace us with your presence," Thomas poked.

"I do what I can, when I can."

"Well, you got your work cut out for you on this one," Thomas wanted to add *superstar* but felt like he had already said enough. He took out his pad and got back to business, "Four dead. But so far we have identified seven different types of ammunition. No forced entry- which means our perpetrators were invited to dinner."

Zimmer took note of the uneaten hot wings with lemon pepper sprinkles sprawled across the floor, "Or they found an all access pass."

Thomas had his own opinions, "Clearly, it was a robbery gone wrong. You can see where some drugs were stolen, but they left in a rush."

Zimmer continued to look deeper. "Judging by the trail of blood, they had to… Aight... Let's go through our normal procedures... See if our perps turned up at a trauma center. Run all of those blood samples- if we are lucky one of our shooters has a violent past... And I'm not sold on the just another robbery angle.

Even the beat cop knows that crack houses aren't welcome around here. This could be a message. Let's look for the gatekeepers."

"Should we take another go at witness statements?"

"Naw... Let's just get patrol to beef up their presence. Maybe we will catch somebody with their pants down who will strike a deal to pull them back up," Zimmer swallowed, "This won't be an open and shut case. It's gonna take hard nose detective work and somebody to slip up."

"We on it." Thomas felt instructed.

Zimmer had already zoned out. He walked the room. Zimmer stopped at each fallen ghost. He examined where the bullets entered and exited. Each body had its own story. Zimmer needed to visualize the shoot out.

He closed his eyes, and his surroundings started to spin. The visuals were intense: Keisha shot back through the bathroom door... Smoke blasted from the back... June popped in the head at close range... Somebody escaped from the front door... Dope was missing. But not all of it stolen, which meant it was an afterthought.

Zimmer opened his eyes. He knew he was dealing with more than a simple robbery and now he had to prove it. He washed his hands over his face... he would need more than his own powers for this one. Whoever he was looking for would not be easy to find.

CHAPTER TWELVE

The cluster of abandoned warehouses that sat on Murphy Drive had always been a tuck-away spot for Mustafa and his crew. When Mustafa and Saif were younger they used to ride their bikes amongst the massive brick buildings, using its rubble to build ramps.

It's where they snuck and smoked their first cigarettes and blunts. Where they stripped their first stolen car. It was their drop off and meet up spot for their *licks*. There was even the rumor of a body in one of the old septic tanks... nobody talked it. Tonight, though, the dilapidated buildings served as a makeshift hospital.

Saif leaned up against the van and smoked a cigarette. He hated mistakes. Saif cut his eyes at Reek, who paced back and forth. Saif wanted to blame Reek for the botched robbery. Reek was in charge of *intel'* and his information was off. The chick in the bathroom was not on the roster.

Reek felt Saif's eyes on him. Reek saw Keisha come in and out of the trap house but never for an extended amount of time. He didn't count Keisha as a factor... definitely, not a factor with a gun.

Reek understood he held fault, but he would not accept full responsibility. He convinced himself if they had alleviated the problem in the beginning, the whole thing would've been avoidable. So, Reek blamed Mustafa. They shoulda struck off the rip, Reek told himself. Not to mention Mustafa's robbery speech… Reek would have shot first. But Mustafa always had a greater purpose.

When they first arrived on Murphy, Mustafa took the needle and sutures from Black, and stitched himself up. The stab wound wasn't too wide or deep thanks to Rico's designer switchblade. Having to endure the pain of the stitches made his mind go blank, and a clear mind helped for sound decisions. After his self-conducted surgery he sat in the van, with the door open, and fingered his dhikr beads.

The crew was usually more precise in their execution. They had been leaning on drug dealers and other parasites for years. It wasn't out the ordinary to slap somebody around with the steel. People got shot… it was part of the game. But four bodies- right after Imam Yusuf got popped. Mustafa dhikred faster. He focused on Allah's Mercy…

ir-Rahim

ir-Rahim

ir-Rahim

Mustafa didn't have time to play the blame game. For Mustafa, the next move was more important than what happened in the past. He lived his life with the next five steps in his frontal lobe. He prayed for solutions.

Black finally emerged from the building, dressed in doctor smocks. Everybody froze in place… and tried to read Black's facial expression. Whatever he had to say they wanted know in advance; there had been enough surprises for one night.

Mustafa wasn't patient, "So, what da deal?"

"Well, he's going to live, that's for sure," Black was matter of fact.

"Al-Hamdulillah," Reek exclaimed… for both of their sakes.

"Yeah, the bullets went in and out," Black continued as he loaded up his car and went through a bag of medications, "Didn't hit any vital organs. But he lost a lot of blood. And he's going to have to recover. These should take care of tha pain. Antibiotics to keep the infection down. And he needs to change tha bandages… I put some topical cream in there for both y'all, feel me."

"Bet," Mustafa smirked. Even with Black's college education. Medical Degree from Morehouse School of Medicine, Dr. Kareem Mohammad was still Black from the Eastside.

"So, where you going to take him?"

But Black wasn't a street nigga. And even though he wasn't a snitch either, there was certain information that didn't need to be shared. Mustafa believed in everybody sticking to their lane. He looked away, and then wobbled onto his damaged leg.

"Black, once again you came through, akh," Mustafa had pulled something out his pocket and hid it in the palm of his hand, "Glad one of us was payin' attention in school."

Black took a look at the money and shook his head, "I'm good… We crew- always."

"Naw, take that. I know we folks." Mustafa meant no disrespect. Black, Mustafa, Saif, and Shim had known each other since Pre-K. Now adults, Dr. Black ran an in-home emergency care service. And Mustafa always bought him business. Mustafa paid his way.

"How ya momma doin' over there?" Mustafa changed the subject.

"She good... Asked 'bout you tha other day."

"Yeah... I been tryna get over dere to see her since your dad's Janazzah. You know, Bro. Umar was my man. Big blow to da community."

"From Allah we come, to Allah we return... right?"

"Mashallah."

Small talk wasn't necessary, but it eased the situation; reminded them of their brotherhood.

"Well, I'm going to get outta here," Black realized there was more pressing matters on the table, "Y'all hit me up if you need me."

"Slaama-Laikum, Bruh."

"Wa-Alaikum-Salaam."

Black gave the rest of the crew the greetings, and they returned the salutation. They watched in silence as the car pulled off. It was like watching a part of your life drive away.

Once Black's pitch-dark Audi A-8 was out of sight, Mustafa recaptured their attention; "We need to get Shim out of town tonight. Somebody find out he shot and it won't be long before we all on the run."

Saif was with him, "Where you want me to take him?"

"We still got akhs down there in Valdosta... That way he's close to the border in case some shit pop off, but not too far to get at him, if he need us."

"Yeah... Aight I got that."

"Come right back though... Absence breeds suspension, feel me? And torch that van, akh... gotta kill that DNA."

Saif understood. He thought of the angles. But Mustafa verbalized the steps much better.

Mustafa turned to Reek, "How much work ya come outta dere wit'?"

Reek shrugged his shoulders like he didn't understand the question, "I 'on't know... 4 or 5 bricks maybe."

"Okay." Although Reek could eyeball work, Mustafa didn't have time to point that out. "Figure out what we got. Find somewhere to put it. We 'on't need to play dat card just yet."

"Oh, I got it," Reek rubbed his hands together.

Mustafa ran through several scenarios in his head, "Somewhere oder dan Rashida's house."

"Akh, I got it."

Mustafa couldn't let it go, "I'm serious, Reek, I 'on't need her chimin' in on dis one."

Reek didn't want to cause an argument. He preferred to have the dope in his possession, "Wallahee, Mustafa- I got it."

Mustafa hated when people swore to God. "Aight... Well, it ain't no need to piss in a cup and call it lemonade. Dis shit 'bout as thick as it get. Gonna be more heat than we already got. We gotta lay low 'til dis lick come through wit' Levison."

Saif seemed surprised. "So, dat's still on?"

"Gonna have to be," Mustafa was thinking exit strategy, "Ain't no tellin' how dis gonna play out. We might need dat."

Reek and Saif agreed.

Mustafa limped to his car.

"Mustafa," Saif called after him.

He looked back. Both men examined each other's faces.

"We'll be aight, huh?"

"In-sha-Allah," was the most honest way for Mustafa to answer the question.

CHAPTER THIRTEEN

"With over a week of investigation, police have yet to uncover any new leads in this violent quadruple homicide. We spoke with Detective Zimmer, known in the West End as the detective who captured their religious leader for the alleged murder of two Fulton County deputies. And this is what he had to say," Phaedra stood in front of the boarded house and waited.

Viewer's watched Detective Zimmer speak from the police station, "I want to be clear in no way are we targeting Moslems or the West End community. They are a part of our society like everybody else and like everyone else they will follow the laws of the land or pay the price. Whoever is responsible for this viciousness- we will find them."

Phaedra endured the typical ten-second-delay, "And there you have it, Bill. Detective Zimmer was clear that Atlanta's homicide department is looking into some leads connected to the drugs and DNA found on the scene. But wouldn't give any details beyond that."

Mustafa couldn't believe, how in less than two-months time, he had been so closely connected to the Breaking News stories.

"So, have they found any link between the killings and the alleged murder of the deputies by Imam Yusuf," Bill, the newsroom reporter, asked.

"There has been no direct link just yet. But I am told homicide is not ruling it out as a possibility either," Phaedra had learned to answer a question whether she had the answer or not.

Mustafa shook his head at the methods news media used to sensationalize facts. How were they going to link what happened on Holderness with an incarcerated man? *Just another thing to discredit the religion*, Mustafa thought.

"Thanks Phaedra," Bill turned to the next camera and continued his show, "And as police scramble to solve the murders in the West End, protestors gather downtown to express their displeasure with, exactly, how the police are carrying out their duties. We go live to Ralph McGill at Woodruff Park."

Mustafa found protestors amusing. But before he could enjoy the entertainment, there was a knock at his door. Mustafa wrapped his dhikr beads around his wrist and grabbed his .45 off the counter.

Another knock. Mustafa turned down the TV. He had not left his yard since the robbery. And he entertained no visitors either. He crept to the front door and looked out the blinds.

Another knock.

Mustafa stared through the peephole. He recognized the face, but he didn't put down his weapon. In his current state of mind, familiarity didn't equate to safety. When Mustafa cracked the door, he looked at Reek… but then he looked past him. He needed to make sure nobody was lurking.

"You good?"

Reek looked around. He hated how paranoid Mustafa could get; to Reek it was almost comical. Reek had no fear of getting caught or getting shot or whatever it was that kept Mustafa up at night.

"It's all well, akh," Reek said after he realized Mustafa would not let him in the house without a response.

Mustafa slowly opened the door- his gun on the ready. He had never been down the road. After 18 months on Rice Street, Mustafa vowed if the government wanted to rob him of his time, they would have to bring him in on a stretcher.

Mustafa locked the door- checked the window and the peephole- and put his gun in his waistband, "Slaama-Alaikum."

"Laikum-Salaam," Reek dapped Mustafa, "You on high alert, huh?"

Mustafa didn't care about Reek's judgment. He believed paranoia was tied to instinct. Mustafa just shook his head and looked over at the news. The news reporter was broadcasting live from the rally.

Mustafa grabbed a container of dates and offered one to Reek. It was customary to offer a guest in your home something to eat or drink. It was *the way of* The Prophet, and Mustafa tried to follow The Prophet's *Sunnah*… even though he knew he fell short in some areas. Reek took a few of the dates.

And then Mustafa answered his question, "Yeah… heard Zimmer on da case. He da one got Imam Yusuf… ain't nuthin to play wit'. Phones and all dat shit dead, akh."

"I peeped what it was when dem younguns came and got me."

"Yeah," Mustafa was done with small talk, "You weigh that work up yet?"

"Um... Yeah... Hell yeah." The abruptness of the question threw Reek off. He took a bite of the date to slow his tongue down, "Yep. Already took care of dat, akh."

Mustafa waited for Reek to complete his statement, and became agitated when it seemed like they had to play a game of twenty questions, "So, what it come up to?"

"Shit... A few zones short of three whole ones."

"That's it?"

"Yeah," Reek sounded unsure, "Well, actually, two short. My bad I weighed it up twice. And it was...um... right at 106 zips."

Even though the horrid details from Holderness were vivid in Mustafa's mind, there were certain details that were sketchy. Mustafa wasn't paying attention when Reek hit the stash spot, so he wasn't able to challenge the amount; the quantity didn't match Reek's initial intel. But then again, nothing did.

"Aight... You know where to bury 'em?"

"Bury 'em?" Reek couldn't believe what he was hearing, "I know where to move 'em!"

"Naw," Mustafa wasn't in the mood to go back and forth, "Dat ain't the play."

"Why? Cause of dat shit dem khafirs talkin' 'bout on da news?" Reek challenged, "C'mon akh, I'm tired of basin' my movements on dese devils... Shit feel like we being scary, shawdy."

Mustafa felt *tried*. He remembered Reek had never learned the practice of thinking 5 times before he spoke. So, Mustafa tried to find the words to check Reek verbally. He didn't want it to go any further.

Mustafa looked Reek squarely in his eyes, "Lemme tell ya some'in'... Dere's a difference between being scared and being smart. Ya think if dese folk can pin a murder on da Imam they give a fuck aboutchu or ya fuckin' personal jihad?"

"Akh, I'm just sayin'...."

Reek's attempt to justify his statement made Mustafa angrier.

"I heard what ya fuckin' said," Mustafa's use of profanity was purposeful, "And I'm sayin', I called the play. And dat's dat."

He stepped closer to Reek, "And, Tariq, I fucks wit' you, but don't ever come out ya mouth and call me no coward... at the end of the day, nobody holding ya hostage, bruh."

Reek had no fear, which was foolish, but he wasn't a complete fool, either. The last thing he wanted to do was catch a fade with Mustafa. Reek chewed his date, and combed his mind for a way out of his current predicament.

"My bad, Stafa," Reek apologized.

Mustafa accepted an apology as sufficient compensation- for the time being. There were more pressing issues, and he didn't have time to dissect Reek's sincerity. He stared at the TV.

"Okay.. I gotta go meet wit' Bro Abdullah. You know where to bury it, right?"

"Yeah." Reek had disconnected.

Mustafa could sense something was still off, "Ya good?"

"Al-Hamdulillah." Reek thought it was a perfect opportunity to inject a little Arabic into the situation. "It's all good."

"Aight... Well, let me get ready to get outta here."

Reek nodded and walked back to the door to put on his shoes. Mustafa watched him. He knew Reek wasn't happy about his decision. As Reek grabbed the door handle, Mustafa gave him the greeting of peace, "Slaama-Laikum."

Reek's mind was somewhere else and he didn't turn his body, "Laikum-Salaam."

CHAPTER FOURTEEN

Ayanna saw the news trucks and reporters on the peripheral of the demonstration... just outside the park... close enough for the protestors to be in frame. But far enough to take cover... *should the unruly niggas get riled up*. Ayanna wondered what the so-called journalists were broadcasting to the world.

Ayanna grew up around overt racism. Blatant bigotry honed her detection skills, and Ayanna detected passive-aggressive forms of oppression from a mile away. Ayanna refused to turn a blind eye to the games of politics and the media.

From an early age, Ayanna developed an utter distaste for bullshit and double talk. It started with the doctors and institutions that experimented with her mother's mental health. The red tape her family had to endure, establishing her mother's quality of life, was inhumane. Ayanna learned that America- or capitalism disguised as a free country- boiled down to the bottom line.

Her realization uncovered other inconsistencies in the American social structure. Mental healthcare merged with the penitentiary system. The judicial system locked Black men away for indentured servitude instead of rehabilitation. The more she studied, the more her small town teachings of conformity angered her. And Ayanna searched for ways to speak out.

Ayanna, in her explorations, met and briefly dated, a political activist named Sundiatta Williams. The name of his organization was P.T.P., an acronym meaning Power To People, but could be translated to Pop The Pigs, depending on the occasion.

Ayanna supported her peers, who attempted to leave the world better than they found it. After all, Ayanna came of age in the 1990s, which was a period that celebrated Black opulence and had transformed Black culture into a lifestyle self-absorption and entitlement.

Eventually, her and Sundiatta split because Ayanna *wasn't down* with every aspect of the movement. Ayanna required stability, and the inconsistences between talk and action, in the revolutionary movement, was too frequent for her taste. But she needed a way to be active and allow for her voice to be heard. So, she still came out to support.

Ayanna concentrated on pushing the reporters out of her mind. She was nervous about obsessing over things. Her natural personality was compulsive, and Ayanna remained conscious of anything that could morph into a mental defect. A parent's example sometimes pointed in the opposite direction.

Ayanna redirected her focus to the protestors. The number of demonstrators was small compared to what Ayanna imagined it would be. But in the 21st Century, marches and rallies were out of fashion, unless there was a national headline that went viral.

Yet the energy was high amongst the 25 people who occupied the corner of Woodruff Park. And with Sundiatta spitting his seething rhetoric through the megaphone, the bustling traffic of downtown Atlanta took notice... even if it was on their way to something more important.

The foot-travelers stopped and read the protestor's signs. Ayanna passed flyers to the pedestrians. There was no overwhelming interest, and curiosity was often short-lived. But Ayanna stayed optimistic. Like most of Ayanna's actions, she did what she did for the greater reason behind it.

Across the park Ayanna couldn't help but notice the lean figure that limped down the sidewalk. Something about him seemed magnetic. As he got closer Ayanna purposely placed herself in his path and held out a flyer.

"No justice- no peace, Brother. Let me give you some information about police brutality and freeing our political prisoners."

Mustafa paused before he accepted the handbill. He read over the information on the flyer and wondered who wasted such a great design on nonsense. Mustafa looked at the protestors.

"No justice! No peace!" They screamed.

Mustafa chuckled at the poor little Negroes, recycling the passivity of the past. The truth was Ayanna's beauty captured his attention, and if it weren't for her splendor he would've kept it pushing.

"Something funny?" Ayanna was always on the ready to battle ignorance and to teach the unconscious.

Mustafa realized Ayanna was offended. He heard her battle

stance. Ayanna's passion intrigued Mustafa.

"It just seems," Mustafa spoke carefully, "like we been doin' da same chants forever. And... still it ain't no justice or no peace."

"So what," Ayanna contested, "Just act like nothing is happening? Is that the solution?"

Mustafa smirked. He didn't want to make mockery of something so positive. But he knew better, "Naw... Da solution is to control our communities. If I govern myself den I 'on't need nobody else to govern me, feel me?"

Ayanna considered Mustafa's words. She heard truth in what he said. His words were strong. Mustafa made Ayanna soften... it was a new experience.

"The question is," she checked her tone, "are there enough strong men left to govern us properly, Brother?"

"I know you 'on't buy into dat myth... Sister." Mustafa stared into Ayanna. He expected an answer. He could see her brain racing and was interested in what would come next.

Mustafa's quick response left Ayanna speechless. Did she believe the myth? Had she become cynical about her brothers... And if so, what was she out her fighting for? Ayanna's heart pumped; the stranger challenged her thought process with a single question. Smart was her sexy.

Being mentally dominated aroused Ayanna. The fire and strength in the strange man's eyes stirred something inside her. Ayanna became anxious... the butterflies of allure. She smiled and looked away.

Mustafa, true to his nature, zeroed in on his prey, "Your head-wrap is fly... I didn't get your name."

"Ayanna... My friends call me Yani." The last part of her statement was an invitation.

"I like Ayanna... Means beautiful flower, right?"

"In Arabic," she blushed. She decided not to share the more personal significance.

And then Mustafa asked, "You Muslim?"

"I'm a believer." She submitted her will to a Higher Power, which was a general description of a Muslim.

"In what, dough?" Mustafa's question was blunt.

And once again, Ayanna felt tested. Her walls went up and the proper guards took their positions. "The fact that I believe in something should be enough."

"Not really." This time Ayanna's fury didn't seem as attractive. "It's a lot goin' on out here. You gotta be careful what you believe in." Mustafa handed back the beautifully designed, useless piece of paper. "You be peaceful."

And just like that, Mustafa was done wasting his words. He pushed on.

CHAPTER FIFTEEN

The line had turned into a crowd. And a crowd could turn into a mob; depending on what direction they were pushed. Black folk understood fresh fried fish was not, necessarily, fast food. But Bilal's high volume of business dictated that service moved at a rapid pace.

Ayesha could feel the patrons' impatience. Their annoyance was non-verbal- rolled eyes and heavy sighs. But it was en route to outward cries of intolerance.

Ayesha looked toward the kitchen. The two cooks struggled to keep up with the Saturday afternoon rush. Bilal's Ultimate Fish sat on the border of Atlanta and East Point, and was a staple for everybody within a ten-mile radius. It had long been a hotspot for all Muslims in the Atlanta Metropolitan Area.

Fried fish and bean pies were accurate stereotypes for the Muslim community. Since The Seventies Black Muslims made profit from fresh whiting, trout, and croaker. And Bilal's was the first in Atlanta.

They were the inventors of The Ultimate Fish Sandwich. Two big pieces of fried whiting on a wheat roll dressed with lettuce, pickles, cheese, and homemade tartar sauce. The hot sauce sat on a side counter so the customers could add their own heat.

"How long on tha 20 piece whiting?" Ayesha hated to stand at the counter- looking fabulous in her uniform- while people were unhappy with their orders. She liked the social aspect of her father's restaurant, and unhappy regulars made her hours feel more like work.

"It's coming," the veteran cook tried to reassure her. His job was final assembly, but with the new cook running behind there was nothing to put together. He nodded towards his kitchen mate, who struggled to keep pace. It seemed no matter how hard the newbie tried; he couldn't keep the fryer filled fast enough.

The new fish- all pun intended- caught Ayesha bucking her eyes at him, as if to say, *hurry your ass up*. He labored hard but couldn't handle the volume. "It's coming," he barked in defense.

Ayesha shook her head. She wanted the consumers to know she was on their side. "It shouldn't be dat long," Ayesha tried to reassure the simmering mob. But she didn't know how long before the crowd erupted.

And then just like the superhero Ayesha considered her father to be, Brother Abdullah emerged from his office. His walk was more of a strut- a remnant from his pre-Muslim life. Brother Abdullah smiled and waved at the customers, but immediately picked up on their frustration.

"What's going on?" Brother Abdullah's calm always came across as contrived.

"New Cook cain't keep up."

The newbie heard Ayesha throw him under the bus and shot her a glare. The look was further proof he was out of his league because Bro Abdullah was there to catch his stare. And every body knew that

Ayesha was off limits- in every way.

"I 'on't know what you lookin' at her for!" Abdullah exposed his charade of tranquility. He made his way to the kitchen; his movements indicated danger. But Abdullah recomposed himself and grabbed an apron. "Get from behind my line. Go out back and break down some boxes or somethin'."

New Cook realized that it would be in his best interest to move quickly. But his ego wanted save him from complete emasculation. So, he sucked lips and jerked his body. But didn't engage Abdullah eye to eye. A smart move because it wasn't wise to stir the cold hearted killer.

Abdullah watched the mouse retreat, and then turned to the customers and softened, "Food will be out shortly. Sorry for the delay. I'm gonna take care of y'all."

As Bro Abdullah went behind the line to command his vessel, Mustafa entered. He sized up the room and made his way to the side of the crowd. His separation allowed Mustafa to keep his eye on every body, while remaining inconspicuous... It was how he created invisible.

Ayesha saw Mustafa, though. And instantly smiled. She looked back at her father to make sure he was busy. Abdullah had the laser focus of a hustler and concentrated on assembling and packaging his product.

"As-Salaamu-Alaikum, Mustafa," Ayesha's tone was flirtatious.

"Wa-Alaikum-As-Salaam," Mustafa kept it cordial. He was aware of Ayesha's infatuation with him. And Mustafa was also conscious of

Ayesha's exquisiteness. Her skin was the color of sunburned sand. The fullness of her lips. Her hazel eyes. The drizzle of freckles that decorated her cheeks. She was stunning. Mustafa darted his eyes to the ground. He didn't want to lust after her.

Ayesha would not let Mustafa get off that easy. She checked her surroundings again to make sure nobody was paying attention to her. And then she leaned over the counter and made Mustafa the center of her attention.

"Mustafa, how come every time you speak to me you turn away?"

Mustafa hated to be put on the spot, "Lowerin' my gaze... ain't that what I'm suppose to do?"

"Not when I'm tryna to get you see me," her statement was direct, and it didn't give Mustafa an easy way out.

"I would think especially then," Mustafa had no problem with directness.

"20 piece whiting... pick-up! Ultimate Fish... pick up," Bro Abdullah screamed from the kitchen, "C'mon Ayesha."

"I'm comin'," Ayesha licked her lips and kept her eyes on Mustafa, "Your homeboy is out here waitin' for you."

Bro Abdullah looked up with a frown. He couldn't imagine who his homeboy would have been. And he hated to be pulled out of his zone when money was on the table. But when Abdullah saw Mustafa, he smirked and nodded.

Ayesha bagged up the food and handed it off to the customers. Her father kept putting the orders up and she pushed them out...

and Ayesha seductively glanced at Mustafa, every chance she got. His discomfort gave her a sense of satisfaction.

"Here y'all go... Thanks for waiting."

Mustafa turned in Ayesha's direction as she passed out the last bags. She is gorgeous, he thought. But before Mustafa could lower his gaze, Ayesha caught him peeking. She grinned.

"As-Salaamu-Alaikum, young man," Bro Abdullah startled his daughter.

Mustafa was thankful for Abdullah's sudden appearance. "Wa-Alaikum-As- Salaam."

The two men embraced each other... touching cheeks three times.

"Ya hungry," Bro Abdullah asked and without waiting for an answer turned to his daughter, "Ayesha bring us a couple of sandwiches over to da table."

"Yes, sir," Ayesha answered. From behind her father, she winked at Mustafa... the danger turned her on. Her advances were small compared to society's standards. But bold for a Muslimah raised under the watchful eye of her Abu.

Abdullah ushered Mustafa to the table by the window. The two men took a seat and Mustafa stared at the passing traffic. Bro Abdullah studied Mustafa's face. Mustafa panned back to Abdullah and returned his glare.

Mustafa became the man of his house after his father disappeared. He developed a determination for survival and self-preservation that could only be grown *from the mud*. One of the first older akhs to recognize his drive was Bro Abdullah. He took Mustafa under his wing.

Bro Abdullah was formerly Bruce Jones from Philadelphia. In the late 1960s, Bruce was part of a group of brothers called the Dark Mob founded by Willy Chambers. The organization made money extorting drug dealers and sticking up crap games.

Targeting narcotic peddlers made sense because people in the community had no desire to come forth and speak on the behalf of the poison pushers. And the police weren't too concerned if one more street urchin came up dead or missing.

But in the early 1970s, The Black Muslims developed a stronghold in Philadelphia. The Dark Mob didn't out muscle or intimidate the Black Muslims like they did other groups. So, the two factions merged. Willy became Syid Habeeb and Bruce changed his name to Abdullah Jihad. And they bought righteousness to their profession.

Including religion into their business dealings gave them an extra level of protection against the Feds. The racial tension of the times drew attention to the government's unfair treatment of Blacks. To add religious discrimination would have been catastrophic. Government officials couldn't outwardly target one's right to practice faith. Mosques became perfect hiding spots for guns and money because of the scrutiny law enforcement would face if they raided a house of worship.

The transition from The Nation of Islam to traditional Islam bought about many changes in how Muslims and Mosques conducted themselves. But every body didn't embrace the conversion.

There were brothers stuck in the poorly constructed boundaries of right and wrong... boundaries that crumbled once money became involved . Brother Abdullah was one of those men, and he passed the philosophy of the old regime down to Mustafa.

Mustafa was a sponge. He listened when Bro Abdullah talked about the glory days and how men governed themselves. Mustafa studied his history and taught it to his peers. And as he and his crew came of age, they developed their own government.

"So... how ya doing over dere?" Abdullah already knew the answer to his question.

"Mashallah... it's been busy. A lot of activity," Mustafa was careful with his tongue, "People on patrol searchin' for whateva dey can find."

Abdullah spoke his language, "Yeah... the conversations everywhere."

"I' been listenin'..."

"Just seems sloppy... 'specially for you."

Things had got out of hand. Outside of Abdullah and Mustafa's professional relationship, Abdullah was close to the Imam and a higher authority at Al-Ruh. It was Abdullah's responsibility to speak on the situation.

"Yeah... wasn't nuthin' I could do," Mustafa wasn't used to justifying his actions, "Intel was off... had an unexpected guest.... Turned the party out."

"The girl?" Abdullah's question was rhetorical. He gazed out the window as if he was looking at a different world. "Khafirs let 'em be outta place... Ain't no order in dey world."

They both thought about the statement in its totality.

"So, y'all shut down?" Abdullah wasn't sure of the answer.

"Naw," Mustafa was married to the grind, "gotta work. What ya got?"

Abdullah's slight chuckle was in reverence to Mustafa's hutzpah. Bro Abdullah checked to make sure nobody was in earshot and he leaned in, "Counterfeiters. Jamaicans. Already got buyers. But dey close to home."

"How close?" Mustafa didn't want to beat around the bush.

"Ralph David." Abdullah stared at Mustafa. His glare warned Mustafa of the situation's seriousness... the gaze told Mustafa that it was wise to be afraid.

Mustafa looked out the window. He searched for confirmation. Mustafa was ready to put all chips in... Four murders weren't just going to go away. Whatever happened Mustafa needed enough money to throw at the problem.

"Lemme take a look at it. Might be worth da risk... been thinkin' about my retirement fund."

Ayesha arrived with lunch. She served her father first. And tried to make eye contact with Mustafa as she set his plate. Mustafa watched the food.

"Can I get you something to drink?" The question gave Ayesha a chance to talk to Mustafa directly.

Mustafa kept it pleasant, "Sweet Tea, please."

Ayesha nodded, smiled and turned to her father, "Abu?"

Bro Abdullah shook his head. His shortness let his daughter know this wasn't playtime. Ayesha got the point and dismissed herself. Abdullah knew she had a thing for Mustafa. But Mustafa showed no interest in Ayesha, and Abdullah hated to see his daughter on the chase.

When he turned back, Mustafa's head was bowed for prayer. Bro Abdullah watched. Wondered why he'd never caught Mustafa cutting his eyes to his daughter. Mustafa finished his prayer, and without looking up, Mustafa took a bite of his sandwich. As he chewed, he realized Bro. Abdullah had been watching him.

"Retirement, huh?" Bro Abdullah wanted to fish. "So, maybe it is time for you to settle down... take this money... start a business... start thinkin' 'bout marriage."

Mustafa snickered, "Naw, I ain't ready for dat yet."

"What you mean? It's half ya faith," Abdullah scoffed, "How you not ready for half ya belief?"

"By da look of thangs I'm still havin' trouble figurin' out tha firs' half," Mustafa said plainly.

"We all works-in-progress, Mustafa," Abdullah preached, "But we have to embrace all of it for it to work. We cain't just pick and choose how we worship. It has been prescribed to us. We have to try and…"

Mustafa adjusted in his seat. He had heard enough opinions about his life for today. But Mustafa respected Bro Abdullah, so he tried to brace himself.

Abdullah read Mustafa's body language. Although, Bro Abdullah had a hand in raising Mustafa; he still respected him as a man. "I ain't gonna talk your head off. You know what you gotta do."

Mustafa appreciated the vote of confidence, "Yeah... Inshallah."

Mustafa wasn't as confident in his own ability.

CHAPTER SIXTEEN

Levison swiped the ball from the tee and watched it soar through the sky. His stroke was perfect, and he was sure the disappearing ball had made its way onto the green. Levison froze in his pose. He learned the game from his father and liked to rub in the faces of his privileged peers. He had killer instincts- whether it was on the golf course or in the boardroom.

Councilman Davis, a fair-skinned well put together Black gentleman, smirked at Levison's antics. A fellow *ATLien*, Courtney Davis was from Southwest Atlanta. He attended W.E.B. Dubois High School, along with the rest of Atlanta's blue-blooded Blacks… sons and daughters of mayors and other high-ranking pastors, public officials, and businessmen. Children groomed for Black-Atlanta's politics. And the concept of Black Excellence.

But instead of the traditional HBCU route, Courtney's parents thought it best for their son to branch out- just in case Black-Atlanta took a turn for the worst. Their insight paid off; the whites were coming. Gentrification was changing the face of Atlanta. And Courtney's college roomie was a cutthroat Jew, who liked money more than morals. Their friendship turned out to be profitable.

Special Agent Finn was an outsider to Levison and Davis' little ménage. He shook his head in disgust. Agent Finn was a military man- even his casual golf clothes were heavily starched, creased, and polished. Finn didn't care for Levison's shenanigans, or the double-tongued language of statesmen and capitalists.

"Like taking candy from a baby," Levison boasted.

"Or real estate in the ghetto," the Councilman fired back.

Levison smirked and handed his golf club to the caddie. The games had begun. Levison knew the round of golf wasn't a social meeting *between old friends*, especially with their undisclosed guest.

Levison pushed the conversation forward, "That, Councilman Davis, was good business and foresight... no ulterior motives there, my friend."

The three gentlemen jumped in separate golf carts from their caddies. Councilman Davis was in the driver's seat, Levison rode shotgun, and in the rear- with a full view of everything- was Special Agent Finn.

"And now the city wants a piece of what I have," Levison was ready to cut to the chase.

The golf carts took off down the throughway.

"Well, actually the city would rather coexist with you, Jimmy," The Councilman campaigned, "Listen, I've known you since you used to funk up our dorm room. And we've both had to do some questionable things to build our place in the world. But this is our opportunity to do something for the city that's been so kind to our pockets."

Levison wanted to vomit in his mouth. The whole concept of the greater good was foolishness. Levison wondered why Courtney pretended to support such a myth. After all, The Councilman was a Black Man in a White Man's political game, and understood America's true religion was numbers and dollar signs. And the greater good for anybody who remotely resembled Davis was low on the list... even in a supposed Black Mecca.

"Courtney, get the fuck out of here. I don't have any blood on my hands to begin with. I am simply willing to do business with the very people you want to tuck away in dark corners," Levison let his statement sink in, "And now those corners are worth something to you. But why should I jeopardize my business dealings for your little gentrification project?"

The question infuriated Agent Finn. He was at the end of his rope with all the word play. There was bigger problems at hand... Airplanes into buildings. Massacres in American cities. Syrian Refugees. Obama. Isis. The Muslims were out to create world domination. Finn's job was to stop them. His newfound position in Homeland Security put Finn on the front line for the War on Terror.

The War on Terror was nothing new; Ronald Reagan declared war on Islamic radicalism after bombings in Beirut took the lives of 241 US Troops. Later in the Bush-regime, George W. adopted the phrase after the attacks of September 11th. But just like the days of the Iran-Contra, there was always more to the story.

"Look, Levison," Finn used his interrogation voice, "this is your chance to help with this investigation or become somebody who's being investigated."

"Is that supposed to be some kind of threat?" Levison

wondered how Finn's tone worked on a mid-level narcotics peddler or a computer hacker, who leaked Ashley Madison accounts. But Levison played for the big leagues, and his money trumped the intimidations of federal agents. "Councilman you didn't brief your henchman on who he was meeting with?"

The question was rhetorical. Levison weighed the level of diplomacy the situation warranted. And then threw caution to the wind. He turned completely in his seat and looked Finn square in his all-American blue eyes, "Agent Finn I welcome your investigation. And what you will discover is that I am connected so far up the ladder that when it is said and done you will find yourself on permanent prescription pill duty in Snellville some fucking where."

The statement rang true. Agent Finn recognized he took the wrong approach with the Jew. Levison was not frightened by America's judicial system. Or deportation. Or waterboarding. Or whatever tactics the US Government used to maintain fear and panic.

"Nobody's threatening anybody, Jimmy," Davis needed to spin the conversation, "Special Agent Finn is good at what he does. So, you don't have to worry about any threats to your business relationships. Isn't that right, Agent Finn?"

Finn hated the political world. He believed he was a part of the guard. And hated to shuck and jive for men who profited from his protection. And then created policy so they could control his job.

"Isn't that right, Finn?" The Councilman repeated himself with more force.

"Yeah," Finn conceded, "My apologies, Mr. Levison... And I can ensure you that whatever you help you provide, the Special Operations Division will make sure it is classified as Law Enforcement Sensitive. By the time we're done covering this up nobody will know who is who... Much less who said what."

Levison looked away as if he was trying to compose himself. Actually, he was gloating in his victory.

Davis decided to sweeten the pot. "Jimmy, look, there's no doubt with Yusuf gone the Moslem grip is waning in the West End... Just like it is no secret the West End is prime real estate. We're just reaching out to our friends to help us move the imminent along quicker... and we won't forget our friends."

Davis pulled the cart onto the green and looked at Levison. Levison nodded. He recognized the subject switched from politics to property and power. And that was the conversation he wanted to have.

"Now we're talking," Levison was back in good spirits. "You tell me that the Mayor is ready to expand the city- I'm fine with that. You tell me that we need to clear the rubble to make room for new development- I can be persuaded into believing that's best. But don't insult me with talks of the greater good and some bullshit War on Crime."

Levison led the men onto the green and took his putter from the caddie, "Talk to me about tax breaks and incentives... That's a language I understand, Councilman."

Levison was in his zone as he mounted the ball.

Davis smirked at his friend's cockiness and Finn's desperate attempt to conceal his repulsion. "You've always been a piece of work, Jimmy."

"Well," Levison's smooth stroke sank the ball, "We are what we attract, Councilman."

CHAPTER SEVENTEEN

1.

Jessie James- no relation to the famous criminal but just as notorious in his small town- was a third generation sharecropper. He gave his granddaughter several tools to carry her through life. Ayanna was skillful and independent. Matter of fact and no nonsense. But the old farmer, also, made her quick-tempered and precise with her hands. Ayanna later curbed those traits as she developed into a woman.

The greatest skill Ayanna's grandfather gave her, though, was the ability to occupy her mind. Ol' Man Jessie trained his granddaughter that when the thoughts of the mind became too overwhelming, skillful hands could ease her mental burdens.

It started with her grandfather and the hours she spent outside between work and play. She helped her grandfather grow the land, and learned to stretch her imagination with the things at her disposal. A stick could give her hours of fun.

Her ability to obsess developed into a business of intricately wood-burned earrings, which she sold through her online store and as a vendor for various events. Not only did the innovative designs make her a decent living; they provided her with the necessary hand movements to keep her thoughts at bay. *Diligent Hands* became

Ayanna's therapy.

Ayanna sat at her workstation and closed everything else out. She was getting her stock together for Jack tha Rapper, a quarterly event that attracted up and coming hip-hop heavyweights. Ayanna usually participated in more *cultural* events, but the party scene attracted a spending crowd. And Ayanna wasn't too righteous for good money.

The distractions with her mother had set her work schedule behind. Fortunately, Brittany was able to get a lawyer to properly represent them, and the ordeal of getting her mother sprung from state care didn't even last a month. But the whole process left Ayanna drained. Once the event was behind her, she'd get some much-needed rest.

Her phone rang. The sudden sound made her jump. Ayanna looked down and saw her sister's home number. She didn't want to break from her task so she sent it to voicemail. The ringing stopped.

And started again.

A back-to-back call meant something important. Her thoughts stampeded her brain. She tried to block out all the worst-case scenarios developing in her head. Ayanna wanted to focus on work, but the ringing was a reality she couldn't escape from.

"Greetings," Ayanna answered the phone. It was her mother on the other end, "Oh… hey Momma… How you doing?"

Ayanna strained her eyes and struggled to hear through her mother's gibberish. She wasn't in the mood. But Ayanna's needs weren't always the priority in the mother-daughter relationship.

"Momma, what are you talking about? No… Britt's not trying to kill you, Momma. No ma'am. Where's Britt at now? Who's there with you Momma?"

The phone disconnected. "Momma? Momma?"

Ayanna stared at her phone in disbelief. She couldn't make sense of the babble. Was her mother in harm? Or worse, were her sister and nephew in danger? She tried to redial the number. She got a busy signal.

This time, Ayanna called back-to-back. But she couldn't get through. Ayanna sat her phone down and tried to refocus her attention to work. But her thoughts were on the impending danger. Her mother's mental state was on the loose.

Ayanna turned off her burners, grabbed her bag, and bolted out of the house.

2.

The eight ball fell into the corner pocket.

Mustafa was a samurai with a pool stick. He smirked at Dread. Dread's charcoal complexion and mountain of black locs made him look like a moving shadow in the dimly lit bar. Dread shook his head-slow at first then more intensely.

"God-doh-mighty!" Dread cried out.

Mustafa wanted to burst out laughing, but there was no need to add insult to injury. Plus, Dread had come through. Mustafa believed in community on all levels.

"Aye, dis what I do," Mustafa tried to soften the blow. For a paper chaser any loss hurt. Mustafa knew Dread's challenge was going to result in a defeat. But Dread put money on the table, and Mustafa couldn't turn it down.

Mustafa scooped the money off of the table, counted out his winnings, and handed 100 back to Dread. Mustafa was merciful. "I 'preciate you. Info was A-1, feel me."

Dread stuffed the money in his pocket and cracked a grin, "B'lieve it... I know ya got me."

The exchanged dap

"Already!"

"I'm gone den."

"Be safe."

Mustafa decided to linger and shoot around for a minute. Pool was one of his early hustles. He loved the game, but rarely made time for things he enjoyed. He had been thinking about changing that.

Mustafa racked the balls as Dread made his way to the exit. Mustafa didn't see Ayanna slide in. Dread held the door for her and was captivated by her attractiveness.

"Thank you," Ayanna politely mouthed.

"Britt said she ain't paying Momma no attention," Ayanna continued her phone conversation as she sat at the bar, "Yas', you stupid. Anyway, I'm about to have a drink and go back and finish these earrings for tomorrow... Whatever... it's happy hour somewhere... Mmm-hmm. Bye."

The sound of the pool balls crashing around the table made Ayanna turn around, and she saw Mustafa. Lost in his thoughts. He circled the table like some sort of Indian tiger. Ayanna couldn't help but watch...

"What can I get you, girl?"

Ayanna was almost upset that the bartender had pulled away from her observation of such a well-built specimen.

"Oh hey. Yeah... Um," Ayanna broke free from her gaze, "Let me get a Heineken and a menu."

Ayanna watched the bartender retrieve her drink and lay her napkin down with a sprinkle of salt. The bartender dropped the menu and Ayanna used one hand to gulp down the early stress of the day and the other to start her meal selection.

"Can I get change?" the deep voice asked from over Ayanna's shoulder.

Ayanna didn't want to turn around. She wondered how Mustafa got next to her so quickly. The tiger metaphor became more relevant. Ayanna finished her gulp and then slowly turned to Mustafa.

Mustafa didn't forget faces, but his plate was full. His thoughts clouded his radar. And Ayanna went unnoticed.

"No socio-political challenges today," Ayanna made herself seen.

Mustafa looked in her direction. It took a fraction of a second to place Ayanna's face. He scolded himself for slipping- now was not the time to be off center. But seeing the beautiful woman again made Mustafa grin, "The rebel without a pause."

"Better than without a cause," Ayanna wondered did Mustafa remember the rhythm of their previous dialogue.

Mustafa chuckled.

"You laughing at me again?"

Mustafa was surprised. Even a slight chuckle wasn't his thing. But there was something peaceful about Ayanna. He wanted to engage.

"Somethin' about you makes me smile," Mustafa admitted.

"What like I'm a joke or somethin'," Ayanna tilted her head, "I amuse you?"

Mustafa threw up his hands; "Don't shoot me in the foot, Pesci."

They both chuckled... a well-needed laugh. Nothing extra-gut busting about the joke; it provided a snicker of reprieve. An acknowledgement that with every difficulty there was relief. And it felt good to unearth the peace with someone else.

Ayanna gulped her beer.

"I see ya already turnt," Mustafa was careful to dismiss the judgment from his voice.

Ayanna almost choked on her beverage, "Now see, what happened was..."

"Don't trip," Mustafa didn't want her to have to explain herself, "It's happy hour somewhere."

Ayanna raised her glass, "Exactly... So you wanna join me?"

Mustafa was usually single-minded, but Ayanna was a wanted diversion. "I got a minute... You treatin'?"

Ayanna extended the invitation; so she took no offense to Mustafa's question. Had it been Yasmeen... the conversation would've ended right then and there. But Ayanna believed Mustafa wasn't a taker. She was comfortable treating on their *first date*.

"Sure... What's your poison?"

"Ginger ale," Mustafa winked.

CHAPTER EIGHTEEN

1.

Mo and Nard waited at the top of the parking deck. Mo smoked his third cigarette in fifteen minutes. He kept looking around as if he would see something different in the large buildings that surrounded them. He was new to making these kinds of deals, and everything that didn't fit into his timeline was a red flag.

"Where the hell is this prick at, man?"

"He'll be here... No way his greedy ass won't bite on these numbers." Nard was the opposite. His veins had turned ice cold from his eight years on the street. He was in his pocket. The deal was going down... After that the relationship would be built, and eventually, it would all pay off.

Nard had learned one key piece of information over the years: dope boys loved money- it had a blinding effect on them. They lived knowing it was not if but when they would get caught. The smart ones made provisions. The majority of them road the wave. And Nard's endless supply of cash was sure to lure any hustler to shore.

Nard looked at his partner and saw Mo's *tells*. Mo was trying to *look hard* and it looked rehearsed. But before Nard could give the rookie some last-minute pointers, Reek's Monte Carlo drove up the ramp.

"Here he is now," Nard quietly announced.

"About damn time," Mo flicked his cigarette and flared his nostrils. He thought he was ready.

Reek pulled into the parking space and grabbed his satchel. His pistol was cocked and on his hip. One of his people from Adamsville told him Nard was *a major playa* from Baltimore. So, he needed to be *ready for whateva.*

Reek had eight bricks from the hit on Rico. After putting three to the side for Mustafa and the crew, Reek decided that he would wholesale two bricks and break the rest down for retail.

Nard- being from north of the mason Dixie line- got hit for five thousand a quarter-key. Reek couldn't believe how easily Nard bit on the price. But his name checked out, so Reek decided it was worth the risk.

Reek jumped out the car and looked around. Nothing out of the ordinary… three empty cars. He looked up at the big building and peered at all the windows. Reek couldn't help but wonder if someone was looking back at him. He blocked it out of his mind.

Nard wanted a brick, but Reek started him off light. He wanted the money, but he decided to make sure he was who he said he was, first. And Reek convinced himself that the feds weren't watching him for a quarter kilogram of cocaine .

Reek turned his attention to his customers. He noticed the anger smeared on Mo's face. He thought about the Ruger on his hip.

"Nard, what' up wit' your sidekick ova dere?"

Nard looked back at Mo. His face was screwed up. Nard wanted to tell him to fix his mug. Instead, he made light of Mo's rehearsed persona. He snickered, "We all good, baby. You got dat dope, tho?"

"Fuck what I got. You got somethin' for me," Reek retaliated.

Mo interjected, "We might... Once you tell us what you got."

"Fuck we playin'... patty cake?" Reek felt tried, "Why is you even fuckin' talkin'?"

Nard needed to step in before Mo blew the deal, "Aye... C'mon... Don't worry about him. We gucci. He just gets a little antsy when he is kept waitin'."

"Keepin' it a hund'ed- y'all niggas need ta be happy I'm here, b'lieve it." Reek would cut off his nose to spite his face. And Mo mouthing off was enough to walk away from the twenty-five. "I 'on't even know y'all like dat."

Nard saw his way in. "Maybe not." Nard cracked-open his bag. "But I am sure you know these guys right here."

Reek broke away from his staring contest with Mo and looked over to the sack full of money. Twenty-five stacks. He forgot about the buildings and the windows. He blocked out Mo's flip little mouth and the two strangers. Reek only saw the Benjamins peering back at him.

Reek wanted to be free from Mustafa's rule... Mustafa's moral criminal enterprise. Reek thought it was foolish that they only robbed dope boys and rappers. But didn't capitalize on the market in their own hood. Mustafa wanted to take the bricks and sell them to white boys and peddle the jewels to his shady Jewish connect.

Reek didn't see the difference. To him the criminal life was just that. He separated Church and State. For Reek the things he was forced to do- as a Black Man in America- had nothing to do with his relationship with Allah. So, he didn't have the guilt Mustafa associated with their lifestyle.

Reek had always had to scrape and scheme for what he considered to be his fair share. So, the fact that Mustafa donated a portion of their earnings to the Ummah, robbed Reek of his portion. Then Mustafa took a larger share as the leader. Even though, there was never an election or a yearly review.

Reek had always seen himself as a boss. But he lacked the ability to make things shake on his own. Reek couldn't figure out why nothing ever panned out. All he wanted was to be the top dog. And he was willing to do whatever it took to get the position.

2.

"You told him to do it?" Saif couldn't believe what he was hearing.

"Yup," Mustafa sounded indifferent.

Saif tried to make sense of it all, but came up with nothing. "You mightta been betta off doin' dat yaself."

"I 'on't even like touchin' dat shit- fa real, fa real." Mustafa ignored Saif's slick reprimand. "Reek come from dat game anyway."

"Exactly." Mustafa's nonchalance surprised Saif. "And what he say?"

"He bucked a lil'- which is understandable... But I made it clear…"

Mustafa stopped mid-sentence and stared across the parking lot at the row of buildings on Ralph David Abernathy Blvd. A brown van with small round back windows pulled in front of the convenience store.

"You see 'em?" Mustafa referenced the two Jamaicans that got out of the van.

Saif stared at the two *dreads*. The taller of the two, Blacka, wore a buttoned down rayon shirt with a pair of jogging pants and *timbs*. Blacka's shorter sidekick, Copper, dressed in a black t-shirt with camouflage cargos. They both looked like authentic Rastas… not the generic knock-offs of the American variety.

The two rude boys walked to the back of the van. Copper stood guard and watched the traffic; his eyes darted across the street. Saif and Mustafa slumped down in their seats. But watched carefully as Blacka snatched up two duffle bags from the back, closed up the van, and made his way to the store. Copper followed him while he kept his eyes peeled for unwanted movement.

"Dese niggas is doin' it in broad daylight," Saif said in disbelief.

"Ain't no reason not to," Mustafa broke it down, "Goin' in ain't nuthin' but duffle bags full of five dollar bills. It's dose fidies dat come out dat's da problem."

The Jamaicans disappeared into the store.

"My connect tells me dat da back door is controlled by da same kinda buzzer Levison dem use," Mustafa painted the picture.

Saif shifted in his seat, he needed to visualize every detail.

"The old man behind da counter controls dat."

"Who's back dere wit' da money?" Saif imagined an armory.

"Just da washer and da printer. Dey try and keep as lil' traffic as possible."

Saif adjusted in his seat, again. The process was foreign to Saif, so he had to use his imagination to visualize the set-up and process...

The Jamaicans where using a traditional bleach and print process. The bills were treated with an advanced bleach solution (that maintained the bills green tint), dried, and then reprinted. Another key to their operation was a large supply of Nigerian Ink that was identical to the US Treasury Department.

The bills where easily distributed because the paper was real. It felt like a bill. And when some cashier took out her little marker and drew a couple of lines on the paper it didn't change brown or black.

The bills circulated throughout The United States and abroad. Jamaicans had a large network of Black Market and legitimate outlets to dump the money. Every avenue was at their disposal- from weed to restaurants. Saif's daydream was interrupted when all four of the moneymakers emerged from the store.

"Dat's dem?" The men were exactly as Saif had imagined them.

"Yep. Dem two pump out half a million at a time. And da other two don't show back up 'til dere's a perfect batch."

"So, when we gonna hit 'em?"

"Batch won't be done for a few weeks... We gonna hit 'em on a Sunday morning, when half da Westside in church and da other half passed out from da night before.

"Hell yeah," Saif watched the Jamaicans drive away, "Easy lick."

Inshallah, Mustafa thought to himself. Truly Allah was the best of planners, even though, Mustafa couldn't figure out how this design would come together. The hit on Holderness still had him spooked.

"Ya heard from Shim?" Saif was assembling the perfect crew in his head.

"Yeah... He good... recoverin'," Mustafa knew what Saif was thinking, "Talmbout tryna get back to da city."

"Fuckin' soldier, akh. Cain't stop dat."

"Hell naw..." Mustafa wondered was there a way to stop any of it.

Mustafa once read a book about the Toltecs- an ancient Mesoamerican culture. They believed mankind lived the agreements he was born into. And that some of those agreements didn't coincide with who a person was internally.

Islam taught Muslims not to be consumed by the Dunya (the spoils of the temporal world). But a man was obligated to earn. He was the provider, and in America doing both seemed like an unavoidable dichotomy... To Mustafa, the agreement contradicted itself.

Mustafa stared out the car window. Lately it seemed like he was always searching for the answers.

"You aight?" Saif could sense something was off with his brother.

"Yeah. Jus' been thinkin' about what comes next... When all dis is ova, know wha' I'm talmbout?"

"Shit... Jennah." Saif didn't hesitate.

"I was thinkin' 'bout a lil' sooner dan dat, Saif... I dunno. Jus' ain't tryna strike fo'eva, feel me?"

Saif didn't feel him. He wasn't one to do a lot of planning for the future. Saif wasn't reckless... not a live wire like Reek. But he was a warrior and warriors died. It was never before their time. All he could do was serve his best in battle. And pray for the best of *the afterlife*.

"Ya stressed?" Saif jabbed, "Maybe you need to get away. Get your head right. Get ya a *mutah* goin' on and lay up wit' somethin' sof' and regroup."

Mustafa loved Saif, but he knew his homeboy wasn't on the search for the deeper meaning of anything. Saif was concrete.

"Cain't say a temporary marriage is gonna solve my problems, akh," Mustafa didn't hide his sarcasm. Mutah was the concept of temporary marriage that, according to Hadith (sayings and practices of Prophet Muhammad), was prescribed during wartime- as Islam was being spread. And Black Muslims used the war on Black Men as the equivalent.

Hadith stood as a principal of belief and traveled through generations like folklore- and remixed with peoples' understanding. Mustafa was sketchy on anything that relied on the memory of man. And Hadith weren't always sound.

"Might not. But you gotta take care of dat stress... You even got somethin' sof' to lay up wit'?" Saif joked

"Hold on, shawdy."

"Naw... I'm just sayin', Stafa," Saif tried to contain his laughter, "ya always grindin'… I 'on't never see ya chase nut'in but dat bread… feel me?"

"Whatever, nigga." Mustafa wasn't one to chase tail. "I just met a bad one da oder day."

"She Muslim?"

"Naw." Mustafa didn't know what Ayanna believed. "On some Black-Righteous-Space shit or somethin'."

Saif's face screwed up in disgust, "Oh hell naw… That'll work my nerves. Pick a side, nigga."

"Aight Reek," Mustafa snickered.

The two men laughed. The more they giggled the more intense it became. Once again, Mustafa needed the laughter. They hadn't laughed like that since they were teenagers. Mustafa eyes filled with tears. The tears released pain. Mustafa couldn't stop. He was hysterical. For some reason he thought of Ayanna.

"Jihad, akhi!" Saif kept the joke going as they pulled up to Mustafa's crib.

The laughter subsided, and the two brothers just sat for a minute.

"So, we good for tonight," Mustafa composed himself.

"Mos' definitely… Nigga, a mark, man. Should be easy like a Sunday morning."

"Aight… Later on den." Mustafa's dap said thank you. He could rarely let down his guard. But Saif was his brother. "Slaama-Laikum, Bro."

"Laikum-Salaam, Akh."

CHAPTER NINETEEN

1.

Atlanta's nightlife was top-notch. It was a place where Black folk partied based on their musical preferences and their tax bracket. *The city too busy to hate* removed the color of one's skin and replaced it with their dress code, educational, and economic status.

404 West was a chic hotspot nestled on what was being rebranded as West Midtown, just blocks way from The Bluff- one of Atlanta's most notorious neighborhoods. The club marketed to an upper echelon clientele, but its location attracted the corporate and the criminal, alike. And the blending of the two was a more accurate portrayal of Atlanta's Black demographic.

Mustafa eyed the crowd. He never understood why people stood in lines and spent their hard earned money to then be shoved into an overheated room packed with drunken strangers. It was an environment built for posers- where music gave club-goers their ego and identity in three-minute increments.

By his nature, Mustafa noticed the women- barely clothed and ready to further weaken their defenses with as many free drinks as their outfits (or lack thereof) afforded them. Naked and drunk in a room full of vultures, was neither safe nor ladylike in Mustafa's strong opinion.

Mustafa and his crew made their way past the line and walked passed the bouncer and the metal detectors. The trio walked into the main area of the club and adjusted their sights to the dark shadows and shooting spotlights. The loud music and the smoke.

It was an erratic environment. The Crew centered themselves and separated from the vibe. They were not there to party. They were on the hunt and that would take concentration.

Up on the main stage Mustafa spotted their target. The rapper, Young Whoeva, controlled the crowd... His entourage, most of them weaker than *the studio gangsta*, surrounded him.

The audience rapped along in zombie-like unison- entranced by Young's song. Most of the lyrics were an insult to the fans: *You broke niggas ain't me... I can fuck your bitch... You hoes ain't loyal...* The list went on.

Mustafa motioned to Saif. Saif nodded and alerted Reek. The master hunters didn't need words, they were all aware of their victim. Reek rubbed his hands together and licked his chops. The eyes of the predators zeroed-in on their prey. Now all they had to do was wait for the right time to pounce. They disappeared into the sea of people... and circled their game.

The night drug on forever. The Crew sat at strategic locations in the VIP section to keep an eye on Young Whoeva. The rapper bathed in an endless stream of groupies and hanger-ons, who hoped to get his attention. Mustafa watched the jewels.

Mustafa's patience had worn thin. He wouldn't have been caught dead in the spot if he weren't working. And the rapper looked like he would party all night. Mustafa needed a break.

So, he whispered to Saif, "Hit me if dis lame do anythang oder dan swim in his own ego." And dismissed himself to the bathroom.

Mustafa pushed his way through the crowd. He didn't like the vulnerability the dark room created. Especially when there were other predators in the mix; Mustafa knew they saw him like he peeped them... no acknowledgement needed.

The restroom area provided Mustafa with the relief he searched for. Logistically, the area muted the music and was cooler than the rest of the club.

"Al-Hamdullilah," Mustafa muttered to himself. Mustafa took a minute to reflect on his God's Grace. He closed his eyes and washed his hands over his face. The 10 second pause put Mustafa right back in his zone. He continued on his path to the restroom.

"Going somewhere?"

The voice surprised Mustafa, and he spun towards it. It was Ayanna. Once again she had caught him off guard. Mustafa didn't believe in coincidences. His paranoia began to poke its head. Mustafa, briefly, wondered if Ayanna was trailing him.

"I scared you?" Ayanna asked playfully.

"Cain't say I'm familiar wit' dat emotion," Mustafa plainly stated.

Ayanna examined Mustafa's eyes. The hardened first layer masked pain. Despite the sadness, a glow of confidence made them sparkle. She saw control and calm. It was clear Mustafa was brave and wild. His eyes were complex, but they lacked fear.

"I bet," Ayanna agreed. "So, you following me or what?"

Mustafa smirked. He was becoming more attracted to their banter, "I was just gonna ask you the same thang."

"I'm up here on my grind, thank you very much sir." Ayanna motioned to her table amongst a small group of other vendors.

The wood burned earrings and accessories were unique and crafted perfectly. They were an impeccable mix of handmade and expertly finished. Although Mustafa wasn't at the club to socialize or shop, the beauty of her work compelled Mustafa to examine it.

"I remember you tellin' me you did dese... But dese are dumb."

Ayanna beamed with pride. She knew her work was great, but something about Mustafa's acknowledgement actually meant something to her. She shrugged it off, "What you thought... I was just stringing together beads?"

Mustafa heard a hint of guardedness. He decided on more flattery. "So, activist, painter, jewelry maker... What don't you do?"

"Bullshit," Ayanna said with no hesitation

The two laughed.

Ayanna liked that Mustafa remembered the details of her life, and didn't want him to leave anything out. "Don't forget I work at the community garden..."

"Right," Mustafa recalled, "Farmer Yani."

Mustafa calling Ayanna by her nickname made their relationship feel intimate and timeless. She blushed.

"So, what you doing up here? You don't seem like the clubbing type."

"I'm working." Mustafa was glad Ayanna could tell the

difference.

"Oh yeah?" Ayanna looked around trying to guess Mustafa's profession, "Doing what?"

Mustafa's cell phone vibrated: WE MOVIN NOW!

"Look, I gotta go," Mustafa didn't have time to answer Ayanna's question, "But we bump into each other again and we gonna have to get married."

"Is that right?" Ayanna inquired. Mustafa's statement trumped the fact that he suddenly had to rush off.

Mustafa had said enough. He winked and spun on his heels. Ayanna watched him leave- both confused and intrigued. It was like the sea of people parted to make way for his stride.

Outside the spot, Reek was the first one out. He bee-lined across the parking lot. The rapper had no idea he was sandwiched in-between Saif and Mustafa. As Young Whoever made his way out the club, the adoration of his fans distracted him. He wasn't big enough for any real paparazzi, but large enough to attract every sack-chaser in The A.

Saif and Mustafa slid by the rapper but kept their eyes on him. They jumped into the black King Ranch F-250. Reek sat in the driver's seat. Saif hopped in the back and Mustafa in the front.

"What you had to shit or somethin'?" Reek's question was more of a reprimand.

Mustafa remained fixated on his victim and cocked his gun, "Make sure you 'on't lose 'im."

Reek glared at Mustafa. Mustafa refused to turn his head. He didn't owe Reek an explanation.

The rapper pulled off. He dropped the top of his candy red Camaro and waved at his followers. Reek, preoccupied with Mustafa's arrogance, didn't notice the movement.

"There he go," Mustafa ordered

Reek darted his eyes back to the rapper and pressed on the gas. Mustafa cut his eyes to Reek. Reek's passive aggressive jabs were getting out of hand, but Mustafa dismissed his thoughts. Mustafa was in go-mode and thought maybe he read too much into the situation.

The matte black truck tailed Young Whoeva. No one talked on the mission... Every man engrossed in the pursuit. Saif caressed his strap. Reek smoked a cigarette. Mustafa stared ahead, his tool on his lap, and fingered his dhikr beads.

Young Whoeva was half-drunk and high and wasn't paying attention to the killers in his shadow. He was too busy rapping along with his own lyrics... And checking his appearance in the rear-view mirror. At one point, he even took a selfie. A man that consumed with his image perplexed Mustafa.

"Istafallah," Reek mumbled.

Mustafa agreed with Reek, but the use of the word always made Mustafa uncomfortable. And he looked away. A homeless man caught Mustafa's attention. The vagrant pushed a shopping cart with a mountain of aluminum cans down the street. Time slowed... something about the man seemed ghost-like and haunting. The image grabbed Mustafa and wouldn't let go.

"Here we go." It was Saif's voice that snapped Mustafa back

into his reality.

Mustafa saw the yellow light. Only a fool would have stopped at the red light that separated Pittsburgh and Mechanicsville. The rapper slowed down. And when the light turned red, the rapper came to a complete stop. He knew he couldn't have planned this better.

"Hell yeah," Reek muttered. "Hold what you got."

He clutched on the steering wheel...

Pressed on the gas...

And... Boom!

The grill of the F-250 crushed the back of the coupe. The unsuspecting rapper jerked and hopped out of his car without hesitation.

"What da fuck?"

Mustafa got out the truck... his shotgun to his side- out of view...

"Damn, Bruh! Y'all ain't see da god damn light?"

Mustafa looked at the bumper, "Shawdy, I think you should jus' calm down."

"Man, fuck calming down. Real talk, dis luxury nigga!" The rapper believed his own hype.

Mustafa lifted his canon and took aim, "Nigga, I said you need to calm your ass down."

The rapper's eyes turned to saucers. This was the first time a pistol had been pointed at him... despite what he said in his lyrics.

"Oh shit," The rapper tried to run... but when Young Whoeva twirled Saif was there to greet him with his two Glock 44s.

"Fuck ya think ya going," Saif pulled back his hammers, "Time to come up out dat luxury, nigga."

The rapper stood frozen and then dropped to his knees. "C'mon shawdy," he whimpered, "Please, bruh... Look..."

Young Whoeva peeled off the layers of diamonds around his neck...

"I swear, bruh, I 'on't want no trouble, man... Fuck da car, man. Ain't nuthin, my nigga..."

The rapper released the jewels onto the ground and emptied his pockets...

"Bruh... I got money... whatever you need. Man, please don't hurt me. Please!"

Saif looked over and sneered at Mustafa. The two gangsters wanted to burst out in laughter. Mustafa rarely listened to supposed *gangsta rap*, because he didn't believe ninety-five percent of rap niggas. And he thought the other five percent were fools for implicating themselves on wax. But he had listened to Young Whoeva's lyrics, in research of the job, and definitely expected a little more push.

Mustafa watched the grown man grovel on his knees. Mustafa rested the sawed-off on his shoulder. He walked over and picked the trinkets off of the ground and handed them to Saif.

"I tell you bruh, y'all rappers are so fuckin' disappointin'," Mustafa scolded, "You would think with all that jaw jackin' y'all niggas would be ready to bus' your guns... But y'all ain't bus'in' shit."

Mustafa put the barrel to the rapper's forehead...

Young Whoeva cringed.

"Check it, shawdy, I 'on't wanna hear 'bout dis shit... Not from da police... Not in da streets... Or in none of your songs, feel me," Mustafa almost felt sorry for the *pussy ass rapper*. But when the rapper bowed his head to the ground for mercy, Mustafa was disgusted. He only bowed for his Lord. And couldn't respect a man who knelt to another.

"Man I promise... I ain't saying shit," Young Whoeva prayed, "I swear on everything I love, bruh."

Mustafa nodded to Saif. And they slid back in the truck, leaving the rapper in prostration. Reek had a grin plastered on his face. He mashed on the gas and fishtailed into the night.

2.

Exhaustion struck Mustafa as he unlocked his front door. The music and the environment had sucked everything out of him. He stopped in his entrance and took off his shoes. He put his shotgun and the bag of jewels down on the counter. And went to the bathroom to cleanse himself.

Mustafa entered his prayer room, his face still wet from ablution. He wrapped his dhikr beads around his wrist and stood at the foot of his prayer rug. Mustafa closed his eyes and took a deep breath.

He chanted in Arabic, "Allah is greatest/ Allah is greatest/ I bear witness there is no God but Allah/ I bear witness that Muhammad is the messenger of Allah/ Come to prayer/ Come to success/ stand for prayer/ stand for prayer/ Allah is the greatest/ Allah is greatest/ There is no God but Allah"

Mustafa cupped his hands for a silent prayer, and then brought them to his ears, "Allah-hu-Akbar!"

CHAPTER TWENTY

Ayanna understood the problems gentrification caused for the Black community, but she loved the new scenery white hipsters bought into the city. There was a time when the streets of Old Fourth Ward weren't safe; now it was one of Atlanta's more progressive communities.

Ayanna and Yasmeen sat on the rooftop patio, overlooking The Oakland Cemetery. The waitress dropped off two pineapple mojitos. Atlanta's weather contributed to the quality of life. Although every season showed its personality, it was common to still have 78-degree days in late-Fall. The weather was bipolar.

Yasmeen stared at her friend. There was a glimmer in Ayanna's eye when she talked about the mystery man. Yasmeen was just happy Ayanna was talking about a man, period. She never comprehended what Ayanna hoped to gain from her bouts of celibacy.

Yasmeen depended on sex for several things. There was a power she found in her pussy. She loved the word... pussy. It had power. Seduction. Comfort and destruction. It provided life and crumbled empires. But its magic depended on its owner. And Yasmeen considered herself a sorcerer.

"It's his eyes... Intense... Like he's looking through me," Ayanna stared at the tombstones. She didn't want to make a big deal out of a stranger.

"And you want him to look up inside you," Yasmeen teased.

"You know what? You need to turn down."

"Mmm," Yasmeen sipped her drink, "for what?"

Ayanna chuckled for a minute and then the laughter trailed off. She stared off to her thoughts. Yasmeen realized her friend had faded away, but she didn't interrupt her.

"I don't know," Ayanna broke her silence, "What do I even know about him... Maybe I'm just looking for an escape. Still looking for some knight on a white horse- in shining armor. Some fuckin' snow white shit."

Ayanna sipped her drink. She didn't want to make eye contact with Yasmeen. She was close to tears. The strong Black Woman narrative exhausted her.

Yasmeen identified with her sister's struggle and reached out to her friend, "And what's wrong with that?"

"Girl, I am too old to be playing those kinda games."

"Right," Yasmeen rolled her eyes, "true partnerships and shit."

"Whatever, hoe, you know you lonely." Ayanna believed in true partnership and all that came with it. And she assumed, deep down, Yasmeen wanted it too.

"Hoe? Anyway!" Yasmeen would never admit her true desire. "I'm surprised you ain't waiting outside the U-Bar to ride Mandingo-The Mechanical Bull, by now."

Ayanna choked on her drink. "It hasn't been that..."

Before Ayanna could get the words out of her mouth,

Yasmeen outstretched her neck and dropped her head to the side.

"Ok... it's been a minute," Ayanna admitted. She jumped on the defense, "I just don't have room for no more bullshit."

"Well, what do you know about him?"

Ayanna shrugged, "I don't know... um... he doesn't smoke or drink."

Yasmeen smacked her lips, "Sounds like he's on paper."

"I doubt it," Ayanna thought about why she doubted it. The fact was she had no concrete proof. "I mean- I don't know. I don't think... So... he's a Muslim."

Yasmeen threw her hands in the air, "Them muzlim niggas is crazy, girl. Fuck around and be walking around here with a mask on your face."

Ayanna blushed, "He told me the next time we ran into each other we were gonna have to get married."

"Wha' da fuck? You like that crazy shit, don't you?"

"I don't know... I thought it was cute."

Yasmeen shook her head. Ayanna was flighty and weird. Yasmeen loved that about her. And she understood if she pushed to hard Ayanna would lean in opposition.

Ayanna was already off to the races. Her face lit up as she remembered the details of Mustafa's architecture. "He's cute... and clever... and strong."

"Well, all that might be well and good," Yasmeen didn't want to destroy the dream, "but I'm trying to tell you- it's no telling what those muzlim niggas be into."

Ayanna thought about what Mustafa was into… The curiosity strengthened her attraction. She fantasized about the quiet warrior.

CHAPTER TWENTY-ONE

1.

Zimmer strutted into the busy police station. He loved his life, and the precinct served as the headquarters of his entire existence. The energy in the station was always on ten. Desks and detectives littered the space. Files scattered the desks. Detectives flipped through rap sheets and reports, worked phones, trolled the internet, and interviewed leads and suspects. And in the case of Detective Thomas, sat around and wasted time on the taxpayers' dime.

Zimmer abhorred his partner's lack of drive. He assumed Thomas' phone call had nothing to do with the riddled bodies on Holderness. Zimmer took off his jacket and was ready to roll up his sleeve when Thomas spun around.

"Captain wants to see you," Thomas announced. He cupped his hands over the receiver to not interrupt his important conversation.

Zimmer threw his hands up and cocked his head to the side. He needed more information. It was one of those moments that having a partner steeped in so much apathy, worked against Zimmer.

And in true fashion, Thomas responded, "I can't tell you. He didn't ask to see me. Got some Feds in there. Must be above my pay grade."

"What tha fuck?"

"Heavy is the head, superstar," Thomas snickered at his partners frustration.

Zimmer wanted to say; *my pay grade is your pay grade you lazy shit-only you do nothing to earn it.* Instead, Zimmer put back on his jacket and hit an about face to the Captain's office.

Thomas didn't miss a beat, "Yeah, I'm back baby."

Inside the Captain's office, Agent Finn and Harris sat in complete silence. Captain Harris disliked the Feds. Their arrogance and autonomy. He didn't want Agent Finn to feel comfortable in his house. Agent Finn could not care less; he was higher on the judicial food chain.

Finally, Captain Harris saw Zimmer round the corner and readied himself for an inevitable fight. Agent Finn noticed the Captain's movements and attuned himself, as well. Finn knew hard-nosed officers like Zimmer smelled fear.

Even though the door was open, Zimmer still knocked. Finn cocked his head toward the door. Captain Harris waved in Zimmer… He stood in the threshold and sized up Finn.

"Close the door behind you, Detective," Harris ordered.

Zimmer peeled himself from the doorway. And took a seat next to the Fed. He kept his eyes locked onto the Captain.

"So, what up Cap'?" Zimmer's question was loaded.

"Detective Zimmer, this is Special Agent Finn."

Zimmer gave Finn a half-handshake, but failed to turn in the Agent's direction.

"So, how are things going with the West End case?" Captain

Harris probed.

"It's coming," Zimmer stated, "Not an easy place to collect info. But we are turning hard on it."

"Well, it seems you may have a little help," Captain Harris revealed, "but we are going..."

Zimmer interrupted, "Don't recall saying I needed any help... Captain."

Captain hated the politics of the legal system. Especially when it affected the State's ability to follow its established procedures. He searched for the proper response.

Agent Finn found his opportunity to interject his judicial supremacy. "Whether you are looking for it or not- I am sure- given the current climate of the country, you can understand how certain variables can quickly move something from a local level to a federal one."

"You're going to have to educate me a bit," Zimmer always had a response up his sleeve, "Because a few dead Blacks in the West End seems like business as usual to me."

"Ordinarily," Finn smirked, "But the world is filled with Islamic extremist. And your suspects- who we believe to be involved in domestic terrorism- injured one of our undercover agents. And now our drugs- which were taken from your crime scene- have made their way back into circulation... all of which you have no knowledge of... which should make it easy for you to comprehend why the Federal Government needs to get involved."

Zimmer hated to not have all the information. Finn played with spades. Zimmer needed help. "Captain?"

But Harris was defenseless, "Detective, nobody is saying that you have to suspend your investigation... We just..."

Finn had another two-cent to add, "We are, actually, asking just the opposite. We want you to continue with your investigation... Just hold off on making any arrests... long enough for us to be able to stretch this case further than Mustafa and his crew."

"Mustafa?"

All of a sudden, Zimmer empathized with Thomas.

2.

Zimmer walked back through the station- slightly deflated. He wasn't used to playing second fiddle. Zimmer stood at his desk- comatose.

Thomas could feel Zimmer behind him. And when he saw the look on Zimmer's face Thomas knew he needed to cut his call short... even though he was seconds away from closing his deal.

"Aye, baby, let me call you back," Thomas hung up the phone. He addressed his partner, "I see your pants are still up... I guess I don't need to check your asshole."

Zimmer didn't respond, rather he threw the file on Thomas' desk.

"What's this?" Thomas opened the overstuffed file.

"You ever heard of a Mustafa Karim... call him Stafa in the streets."

Thomas shook his head and then looked up, "Where'd you get

this from?"

"Evidently, these are our new lead suspects. Feds been on 'em for a minute."

Thomas jumped up and threw on his jacket. Zimmer tossed his blazer on the back of his seat and sank to his desk. Thomas looked confused. "What you doing? Let's go snatch these niggas up for questioning."

Zimmer stared with glazed eyes. "Can't... Feds are building some other part of the investigation that is more important...."

"More important than four dead bodies?" Even Thomas had some passion when it came to The Feds trudging on their territory.

"Apparently."

Thomas flopped into his chair, and Zimmer reached across the desk and grabbed the file. He thumbed through the phone book… Stared at the pictures of Mustafa, Saif, Reek, and Shim…. He wondered about who they were and how deep their enterprise went.

Zimmer didn't have Imam Yusuf connected to a robbing crew. But the Feds painted the picture of an intricate terrorist organization, with drugs and murder at its center. And because Zimmer didn't make the suspects first, he had no way of disputing such foolishness.

"You know those two unaccounted blood samples that we pulled?" Zimmer didn't wait for a response, "One of them belonged to one of theirs."

"An agent? He dead?" Thomas new that shit had just gotten real.

"Nope."

"So, what we suppose to do?"

Zimmer chuckled, "My instructions are to build the case from afar."

"And how the fuck are we suppose to do that?"

Zimmer didn't respond.

"I tell you what," Thomas continued, "soon as them Feds get involved..."

Zimmer completed the statement, "Ain't no telling what this shit is about."

CHAPTER TWENTY-TWO

1.

Saif watched Mustafa on the phone. He tried to read Mustafa's facial expressions. Saif could tell something was off. Reek was busy texting on the phone; he showed very little interest in what was going on.

"Aight, we'll see you in a minute." Mustafa hung up the phone. He needed a second to decipher the details of him and Levison's conversation.

Saif grew impatient with the silence, "Whaddup? What he say?"

"Somethin's off," Mustafa broke his contemplation, "Conversation was real loose."

"What you mean," Saif grew impatient, "Like his choice of words?"

"Right," Mustafa spoke more from instinct than provable facts, "Extra, ya know... Like he tryna spell everythang out."

Reek finished his text and checked back into the conversation, "Akh, you been paranoid lately though."

Mustafa didn't have time for Reek's foolishness. He couldn't second-guess his thoughts. His eyes were cold when he cut them in Reek's direction.

With all that was on the line, Reek didn't want to set Mustafa off. He tried to clean up his words, "Wallahee... I ain't tryna say shit... But you might be readin' more into dis... Dat's all."

"Maybe," Mustafa didn't want to misplace his irritation, "I need to look dis devil in his eyes, dough."

"Leh go!" Saif had wasted enough time.

"Well, I'm gonna catch y'all later, Inshallah," Reek grabbed his bike, "I got some bi'ness to handle."

Saif and Mustafa looked at each other suspiciously. They had been so preoccupied that neither one of them had been keeping track of Reek... or the dope from Holderness.

"What you got going on?" Mustafa asked.

"Nuthin major," Reek seemed like he was looking for an alibi, "Just some stuff for my little boy... that's all."

"Oh yeah?" Saif didn't hide his distrust.

"Should I have my lawyer present or something?" Reek acknowledged the skepticism in Saif's tone,

"Aight," Mustafa backed down. Deceitfulness and trickery was Reek's specialty, and Mustafa accepted he didn't have time to filter through Reek's labyrinth. "Well, don't get lost. Ain't no tellin' how this shit 'bout to go down."

"No doubt," Reek recognized that Mustafa glazed over the situation, and it wouldn't be long before Mustafa queried further into his dealings. "I'll holla," Reek got on his bike, "Slaama-Laikum."

Saif and Mustafa both responded, "Laikum-Salaam."

They both watched Reek as he rode off. Reek could feel the eyes on him, and he turned around. The friends observed each other; each searched for a clue to the other's thoughts. The longer they looked the farther apart they became.

2.

It didn't take long for Mustafa and Saif to pull up to Levison's office or make their way through the string of locked doors. Mustafa and Saif entered and scanned the room as if it was their first time stepping foot into the space.

Levison rearranged things on his desk, closed his drawer, and threw his hands in the air like he was happy to see them. Mustafa translated it like Levison had been caught in the act. The question was: caught in the act of what?

"Mustafa and Saifullah, my favorite two Black Muslims," Levison announced their entrance.

Mustafa and Saif's steps stuttered… hearing Levison pronounce their full names came as a shock. Mustafa's eyes darted around the room. His instincts heightened. He looked for cameras or recorders or alphabet boys to jump from behind the curtain. Mustafa shook Levison's hand but didn't make eye contact.

Saif glared in Levison's direction. His kill switch was already activated. Their time for small talk had passed.

"So, Mustafa, did the robbery go well?"

There it was again, Mustafa thought. Levison wasn't a street nigga, but he had made his money dealing with crooks. He knew better than to say anything so plainly. Criminals were always worried about somebody eavesdropping. And part of doing illicit business was proper usage of language. Although the grammar varied by individual and region, a hustler could always decipher the lingo.

"Why you keep callin' me by my full name?" Mustafa spoke direct.

"I keep... I mean," Levison fumbled, "What... what do I usually call you?"

The tension sprouted. Levison looked at Mustafa, and then at Saif... Both glared back at him. And Levison started to sweat.

"C'mon my friend... How long have we done business together? Almost 3 years now, right? You telling me in all that time-I've never called you Mustafa?"

Every time Mustafa's full name sprung from Levison's mouth, Mustafa saw voice recorders and special agents hiding in box trucks.

"Not once," Mustafa asserted, "I always thought it was how you justified our relationship in your head."

Levison seemed to become more nervous. He adjusted a stack of papers on his desk. His mind raced. Levison knew Mustafa was no fool. He decided that it was best to remain ignorant to Mustafa's implication.

"Get the fuck outta here Mustafa," Levison tried to blow Mustafa off, "We've always done great business... You are good at stealing jewels. And I am good at getting you money for them. Nothing to justify."

Mustafa saw the sweaty agents- crammed into the smoke filled box truck. They leaned into the voice recorder; prayed Mustafa would confirm Levison's statement.

Levison was ready to close the deal. "Now what did you bring me from your last robbery?"

Mustafa looked over at Saif.

Saif shook his head.

"I 'on't know what you talmbout." Mustafa played country-dumb. "Anything I put my hands on is from hard work and great connections, Mr. Levison... I'm offended that you assumed it was anything else. I have never said such a thing."

There was danger in Mustafa's eyes, and Levison panicked. "Okay, let's back up here a second, Mustafa... I mean... Muh."

Mustafa tapped his index finger to his own lips. He stared through Levison. His eyes burning and sharp.

The saliva thickened and glued the roof of Levison's mouth to his tongue. The sweat thickened on his brow. Luckily he was sitting down because if he had been standing his knees would have definitely buckled. He felt light headed. And when Saif took a step forward, Levison's heart hammered on his chest plate.

Saif pulled back his shirt and exposed the steel on his hip.

Levison's eyes widened. Bambi in high beams. Nowhere to run now little doe, Mustafa thought. He sneered as he considered the analogy.

Levison had never witnessed Mustafa crack so much as a grin. The smile made him feel faint.

Mustafa realized he would take great pleasure in killing Levison.

Mustafa spoke with his eyes; he didn't know who was listening. He tiptoed with his words, "It's been good seeing you again, Mr.

Levison. Sorry I couldn't help you with whatever you were looking for."

Levison's response was silence.

Mustafa got up from his seat. Saif came and stood by his side. The silence blared.

Levison wanted to call for help, but he wasn't trained on the proper protocol for this situation. He felt like anything he said would incriminate him, so he just sat immobile. Levison's eyes panned from the door to the pistol on Saif's hip.

Saif looked at Mustafa. All he needed was the go-ahead. Mustafa decided the dish would be served cold. Mustafa shook his head. Saif covered the pistol.

"Good-bye, my friend," Saif took great pleasure in the encumbered farewell. Saif was positive he'd get his shot.

Levison was still mute. His eyes followed Mustafa and Saif as they left the office. The taste of vomit filled his mouth. Levison struggled to hold himself together. And as the door slammed shut, he sank down in his seat.

"Fuck!" Levison was talking to whoever was listening.

Mustafa and Saif were always silent whenever they exited the office. But this time the quiet was thick. Both men understood their lives hung in the balance. The hounds were on their heels. They pondered on their weak link.

Levison's involvement meant an investigation bigger than dead niggas on the Westside. If that was all there was to it, the paddy wagon would have already come to pick them up. To Mustafa and

Saif it was obvious the Feds were involved.

They exited onto the busy street. Mustafa experienced sensory overload; he heard every sound. His eyes darted around him. The box truck across the street. The telephone technician. The man in the black business suit- talking on a Bluetooth... The traffic light changed...

"What da move?" Saif could see the strain in Mustafa's face.

Mustafa tried to calm himself. He stood frozen. He caught his breath. "I think I need to slow this down... Go wait for revelation..."

Saif realized his brother had reached his breaking point. Mustafa needed to escape.

"How long you gonna be up there?"

"I dunno... Couple of days," Mustafa didn't want to share anymore information- not even with Saif. "Go spend some time with Khadijah and the kids... Lay low. I'll hit you." Mustafa looked around again. "Slaama-Laikum."

Saif embraced his brother, "Laikum-Salaam."

Saif watched Mustafa walk away... Separation seemed inevitable.

CHAPTER TWENTY-THREE

1.

Rashida squirmed under the cover. Her body still tingled. Sex was a drug for her, and she loved how Reek gave her a fix. Rough and hard. Even when Reek took Rashida into his mouth… it was carnivorous… like he was trying to devour her.

Rashida looked over at Reek, who sat at the edge of the bed lacing up his boots. Even though she loved to be fucked like a whore, she hated how Reek always left once he made his deposit.

"So, what- you just gonna come and dig me out in the middle of the day and dip," Rashida contested. She didn't enjoy Reek's company, but the laws of *keeping it real* forced her to address Reek's constant flight.

"Hell yeah… dat's what a wife is for," Reek lectured. And he grabbed his pistol, cocked it, and put it on his hip.

Rashida's pussy throbbed. There was something about a nigga with a loaded gun that turned her on. She opened her legs and let the sheets fall between her thighs. Rashida bit her bottom lip, "Okay… then tell me what a husband is for."

Reek surveyed Rashida's curves. The sheets did a poor job at covering her body. He could smell her scent. The sweet aroma made the savage in him come back alive. But he had already gotten what he came for, and it was best to leave a woman like Rashida yearning for more. She couldn't be too sure of her power.

Reek sneered and went in his pocket. He threw a roll of money between her legs. Rashida licked her lips as she reached for the bread. She loved when Reek acted like a boss, and a big part of that *was keeping his bitch laced*. Rashida would deal with Reek's foolishness as long as he held the coin. As she fingered the roll of twenties, she had an urge to swallow Reek whole.

"How 'bout dat?" The question was rhetorical. Reek knew exactly what he was doing.

Rashida didn't look up... she kept counting the money. But before she had the chance to crawl across the bed and show her appreciation, Reek disappeared.

Reek paused on the other side of the door. He thought about going back in to test Rashida's gratitude. But he decided he'd fall through later on that night. He knew the level of debauchery would turn up a few notches if Rashida thought there was another pot of gold at the end of it all.

Reek looked up and saw his son in front of the TV. Rashad looked at his father, and Reek nodded. Rashad nodded back.

Reek didn't have time to talk and didn't want to get caught up in another show-n-tell session with Rashad's endless stream of toys. So, Reek whizzed to the closet, by the front door- grabbing an empty book bag, from the counter, on his way.

Reek hunched over in the closet and shielded his stash from the little boy. The secrecy wasn't for the protection of a father for his son. Reek didn't trust anybody.

Rashad saw his father out of the corner of his eyes. But pretended to be distracted by his television show. He wondered what type of treasure his father had hidden in the back of the closet.

Reek retrieved the bag of dope. Rashad recorded Reek's movements. Rashad studied his father's movements. They were urgent and elusive. Reek took two sacks out of his hidden treasure and tucked them away in his book bag.

Reek got up and turned around, Rashad cut his eyes back to the television set. But his father's gaze demanded his attention. And Rashad slowly looked towards his pops.

"You good?"

"Mmm-hmm," was all that Rashad could muster.

"I'll see you later... okay?"

Rashad just nodded. He hadn't figured out what *later* meant. It had no consistency when Reek used the word. Rashad always imagined that his father was a very important man because he was always on the go.... always had somewhere else to be.

"Slaama-Laikum."

Although Rashad knew that word, he wasn't quite sure of its meaning either.

As Rashad's father vanished through the front door, all he could think about was the contents of the closet... And his father's movements. A parent's impact on their child is not always evident, at the moment.

Reek didn't attempt to balance the scales. His life had always been for himself. But he was Rashad's example- whether he ever realized it.

Reek jumped into his Monte Carlo and mashed out to bump his packs.

2.

Saif escaped from the harshness of the world by playing with his kids. His goal was to be a father and a provider. He would never have thought about bringing drugs into his home. He separated the streets from his life. As Saif's son, Jabril, and his daughter, Jennah, crawled on his back, they were the only things on his mind.

Saif nudged and flipped them around, being rougher with Jabril than Jennah. Just as Saif flipped Jabril, a little too hard, and his son bumped his head on the hardwood floor, Khadijah walked in.

"You are gonna make them too rough, Saifullah," Khadijah fussed.

Saif looked up. Khadijah was thick... enough meat in all the right places. Her hips pushed at her loose rayon pants. Her dark skin glowed. Saif playfully referred to her as a more hood version of Clair Huxtable.

Ordinarily, Khadijah stole Saif's attention, except the kids were still on attack. And Saif never dropped his defenses in war. Jabril got flipped again. This time, he caught his head before it sounded off, but his elbows still made a thud.

"Saifullah!"

Khadijah was really happy that her husband was home and spending time with his kids. There was almost nothing more attractive to her. She loved that her son had Saif as his example. But she also relished her role as a nurturer… the mother lion.

Saif snapped his attention to Khadijah's scream and snatched up Jennah. Jabril banged on his back; he still held a grudge from the thump on his head. Saif stood, and Jabril grabbed hold to his leg. Saif carried and drug them both to where Khadijah had taken post. As Saif closed in, Khadijah crossed her arms and braced herself for Saif's aggression.

"I 'on't think dere is anythang as too rough," Saif said a he moved in even closer. "We gotta be ready… And if somethin' happen' to me… they have to be able to take care of my prized possession."

"Possession?"

Saif put Jennah down… she kept swinging… but Abu had his sights set for his next battle.

"I don't recall you having any possessions over here," Khadijah tried to maintain her war face. The truth was, she was honored to belong to Saif. He belonged to Allah, and therefore, giving herself to her man was giving herself to her Lord.

Saif had always honored her. Even when he was young and wild, he never let her witness him out of character. Khadijah knew there was something dangerous about her husband… that he had enemies… and he did not shy away from violence. But to Khadijah Saif was a provider and a protector. She didn't consider questioning his ways.

"Oh yeah?" Saif balled up his fist.

Khadijah watched his muscles flex. The closer he got, the harder her heart beat. "Go 'head on, Saifullah." It was such a blessing for her to be attracted to her husband.

Saif reached for Khadijah. She tried to run, but Saif snatched her up quick. He wrapped his arms around her, and she tried to wiggle away. He disguised his subtle sexual touches into a family game. And Khadijah loved every minute. She thought how after she finished dinner, and put their children to bed, she would show her appreciation… and Saifullah would show his as well.

"Get off of me…" Khadijah broke free, when Saif's strong hands pulled her back and hoisted her into the air. "I'm not playing with you… Saifullah put me down."

Saif suspended her in thin air. But Khadijah was secure. Saifullah would never let her fall.

Saif bounced her like a baby before letting her down. He was cock-strong. A bulldog. And he liked to show off his strength.

Khadijah straightened out her clothes and gathered herself… cocked her head from side to side like she was ready to spaz. "You betta had… before I had to put dese hands on you."

Saif reached for Khadijah. This time he let her escape his grasp. She swiped his hand away. Khadijah jumped at Saif like she would swing. "Stop playin'!"

Saif smiled; to him she was the real gangster. Not only for how she cared for and raised his kids, but also for the strength it took for her to handle him. Saif pulled his thug in for a kiss. They locked lips for a moment and enjoyed the peace of protection and passion. Still in her husband's arms, Khadijah tapped him on the chest.

"Be gentle with me," Khadijah softened herself.

Saif kissed her again. She was certain they would spend one-on-one time once the kids went to bed.

"I need you to go to the store and get me some corn meal," she knew how to take advantage of him

"What you gonna give me?"

Khadijah looked at the kids and then back at Saifullah. She flirtatiously raised her eyebrow and then said… "Dinner."

Saif laughed and reached for Khadijah. This time she escaped on her own. He watched her hips sway back into the kitchen. But remembered she had distracted him. He was at war. He spun around to his opponents.

"Who wants some more of Daddy?"

3.

Ayanna couldn't get Mustafa out of her head. She hoped her walk home would clear him from her mind; so she could have a peaceful night of sleep. Her co-worker beeped her horn, and motioned for Ayanna to get in the car.

"I'm good," Ayanna waved her off, "have a good night."

Truth be told, Ayanna had no desire to rush home. Her house was empty. Ayanna thought she was fine with being single. But the fantasy of Mustafa reminded her of how much she missed companionship.

Ayanna tuned into the rhythm of her steps and didn't see the white Land Rover creep behind her. After a few steps, she felt the car's presence and slightly turned. Ayanna saw the white vehicle but didn't make out the driver.

"Can I give you a ride somewhere, Sis?" The pilot called from his pit.

"I'm sorry," Ayanna kept it moving. "I don't take rides from strangers."

"I wouldn't consider myself a stranger... maybe a little strange but..."

Ayanna wasn't in the mood for games, "Look I don't need a..." And as she faced the vehicle and its driver, Ayanna realized the shiny white car was driven by a true knight; her mysterious, quiet warrior. She broke into a smile. This time it was him who caught her slipping.

Mustafa exited his steed and leaned against his whip.

"What are you doing here?" Ayanna suppressed the sudden urge to run into his arms.

"Ya told me ya worked here," Mustafa responded as if he was exactly where he was supposed to be.

"So, you decided to come and stalk me?"

"Stalkin' implies dat you didn' want me ta find ya."

"Well, I didn't know you were looking..."

"And I had no clue ya were hidin'," Mustafa knew he had her. "You hungry?"

"Slick." Ayanna was happy to be captured.

"Slick, huh? Well, hop in... Let me feed ya."

Ayanna paused as if she was unsure. She wanted to see if her sentinels would arrive. They seemed to be on break.

"C'mon," Mustafa urged, "we got a marriage to discuss."

"Really?" Ayanna cocked her head to the side.

"But we can jus' start wit' dinner?" Mustafa added before her guards were called from their break.

The rhythm of his conversation was perfect. It plucked Ayanna's heartstrings flawlessly. She blushed and then walked to the other side of the car. Ayanna eyeballed Mustafa the whole walk over.

Mustafa sprang in front of her and pulled her door open. He smirked as he secured her in his ride. And thought that maybe he should pay more attention to Hadith.

4.

"You be safe," Nard called out to Reek.

Something about the statement created a pang in Reek's gut. They had already finished their deal... dapped... *Why the extra goodbye,* Reek thought. Maybe Nard was trying to push them closer to a friendship. Mustafa's face popped up in Reek's mind. Suddenly, Reek felt silly. He was being paranoid.

"No doubt... y'all holla back at me." Reek kept it cordial. He even acknowledged Mo. But Mo snarled and spat on the ground.

Reek chuckled because the lameness oozed out of Mo's pores. He hopped in his Monte and stashed his money inside the panel of his door.

Reek watched Nard and Mo pull-off, and then dug through his ashtray for the half of blunt of *loud* he saved for the next play. Reek backed out of his parking space, turned on his music. And just as he put his spaceship in drive, two unmarked cars sped through the Ashby Street entrance of the parking lot.

"Oh shit," was all that Reek could say as he slammed the car into reverse. But just like magic, two more cars pulled in from the Ralph David entrance and blocked him in. Under normal conditions, Reek would've turned into a track star. But there was nowhere to run.

Reek took a long drag of the blunt as he read the various alphabets the gun bearing lawmen sported. ATF. DEA. APD. Everybody had showed up to the party.

"Get out the fucking car now," echoed into the air.

Before Reek knew it, agents snatched his door open. And he found himself slammed up against the car. He couldn't count the amount of hands that grabbed and pulled at him.

Everybody screamed orders… Their knuckles turned white from the tight grips on their service weapons.

"Wha' da fuck," was Reek's last words.

"Shut up!"

"Shut the fuck up!"

"Don't you move! I'll blow your fucking head off!"

"Don't you resist, you moslem piece of shit!"

Reek believed them. It sounded personal. He closed his mouth. And let them slip on his new silver bracelets- even though they always fit too tight. He just closed his eyes and sucked it up. Reek didn't entertain his fear; he had to get ready for what was next.

As Reek blocked out his surroundings, he didn't see Saif drive by on his way to the store. But Saif saw Reek. Saif read the letters, as well. There was nothing good that could come from a gumbo of law enforcement.

Saif's mind raced. He knew they couldn't be coming for the whole crew or else they would have hit everybody at once. Whatever happened was exclusive to Reek. And the first thing that popped into Saif's mind was the work from Holderness.

"What da hell, Tariq?"

Saif decided the best thing for him to do was to keep it moving. And as he watched Reek get roughed up in his rearview mirror, he picked up the phone to call Mustafa... Break time was over.

CHAPTER TWENTY-FOUR

Ayanna rode down the winding country road. The sun hid below the Georgia Mountains, and splashed blood-orange with traces of gold into the sky. Ayanna reflected on the comfort she shared with Mustafa.

The ease in which they talked... or sat in silence. They had a lot in common. And their differences of opinion just made their connection more interesting.

Mustafa's state of the art speakers bumped Portishead. He allowed his mind to go blank. His phone rang; Mustafa had ignored it throughout dinner. And as they made their way into Ellijay, Georgia, Mustafa cut the leash off and put it in his console. Ayanna smiled. The gesture made their time together more special.

Ayanna was somewhere in the wilderness of her mind when Mustafa's white horse slowed down and pulled into a driveway. She looked at the quaint ranch home- hidden from humanity. Suddenly, the butterflies in Ayanna's stomach panicked.

Her evening with Mustafa was magical. An early dinner at South City Kitchen. Dessert at Café Intermezzo. They talked and debated. He held her hand as they strolled through Atlantic Station.

Ayanna filled with schoolgirl giddiness as Mustafa asked her hand in temporary marriage and instructed her to pick out her gift.

She chose a piece of artwork by a local artist for her temporary marriage dowry. Mustafa said a prayer to commemorate their union. The mix of Mustafa's brooding sexiness and intense spirituality made celibacy seem foolish.

It wasn't the first time in Ayanna's life that she had gone home with a man on the first date. But staring at the remote location, she felt peculiar. Mustafa could sense her discomfort and touched her hand.

"You good?"

Ayanna nodded her head. She shadowed Mustafa into the house. Ayanna noted that Mustafa stopped at the door to take off his shoes. He cut on the lights. Nothing seemed out of place. Ayanna couldn't help but think if something happened to her no one would know where she was. She took out her cell phone. There was no signal...

On his way to light the fireplace, Mustafa noticed Ayanna was frozen in the threshold. "Ya okay?"

"Maybe... I shouldn't be here," Ayanna spoke with uncertainty.

"I can take ya home... I 'on't want ya to be uncomfortable." Mustafa's words were true. Him and Ayanna had a genuine connection, and Mustafa didn't want to jeopardize it by ignoring her needs.

"I don't... I mean," Ayanna tried to clarify her position, "I know we have this whole Mutah thing going on... but I don't want you to get the wrong idea about me."

Mustafa took a step forward Ayanna, "I 'on't have any ideas... I sought you out... remember?" Mustafa didn't wait for Ayanna to answer. He took a step closer, "So, if you need to leave, I understand." Mustafa reached for her hand, "But if you decide to stay… it will make me happy."

Ayanna closed her eyes and let out a deep breath. Safety enveloped her. And Ayanna took off her shoes and followed Mustafa to the living room. Ayanna sat on the couch, a comfy charcoal gray sofa. She sank into its coziness. Ayanna watched as Mustafa placed the logs in the fireplace and lit the kindles.

As he got the fire going, Ayanna noticed a huge Quran on the oak coffee table. The cover was exquisite but simple. Emerald green with gold embossed lettering and middle-eastern line art. Ayanna picked it up and cracked its spine.

Just as the fire caught, Mustafa made his way to the couch. But the image of Ayanna cross-legged in his personal space, with his favorite Quran on her lap, was breathtaking. Mustafa sat down beside her.

"You speak Arabic?" Ayanna believed she asked a legitimate question.

"Naw… not really," Mustafa was embarrassed he never learned to fluently speak the language. "I can read it though."

"Read me something."

Ayanna's statement was innocent. And Mustafa felt obliged to grant her request. He took the Quran from her lap and flipped through the pages. It was his ritual to allow the sura (chapter) to choose him. He was patient as he searched for revelation… and then the Holy Book spoke, *Sura Lailah: The Night.*

"Bismillah ir-Rahman, ir-Rahim," Mustafa mumbled to himself... *In the name of Allah, the Most Gracious, the Most Merciful.* It was the opening statement for anything of importance. Mustafa took a moment to make sure his thoughts were pure.

And then in flawless Arabic he read, "By the Night as it conceals (the light); By the Day as it appears in glory; By (the mystery of) the creation of male and female; Verily, (the ends) ye strive for are diverse. So he who gives (in charity) and fears (Allah), And (in all sincerity) testifies to the best, We will indeed make smooth for him the path to Bliss."

Mustafa had no idea that as he read those verses Reek was back in Atlanta being hauled into the police precinct. Or that Zimmer was pulling a late shift and had seen one of his prime suspects being drug into his station.

Mustafa continued with the revelation, "But he who is a greedy miser and thinks himself self-sufficient, And gives the lie to the best, We will indeed make smooth for him the path to Misery; Nor will his wealth profit him when he falls headlong (into the Pit). Verily We take upon Ourselves to guide, And verily unto Us (belong) the End and the Beginning. Therefore do I warn you of a Fire blazing fiercely; None shall reach it but those most unfortunate ones Who give the lie to Truth and turn their backs."

The words gave Mustafa goose bumps. He let the verses sink in. He looked over at Ayanna. Her eyes were closed.

Mustafa continued, "But those most devoted to Allah shall be removed far from it, Those who spend their wealth for increase in self-purification, And have in their minds no favour from anyone for which a reward is expected in return, But only the desire to seek for the Countenance of their Lord Most High; And soon will they attain (complete) satisfaction."

Mustafa sat and thought about what he had just read. He already understood the translation. Lailah was one of his favorite suras. He reflected on his life. Mustafa had tried desperately to balance the paradox.

The looming contradictions of the streets and Islam... The disparaging similarities the men in his community drew between the historical spread of Islam and the contemporary struggle Black Muslims faced in America. Mustafa was so deep in his head he forgot Ayanna was sitting there.

"That was beautiful," Ayanna tried to reach Mustafa in the gentlest way possible.

Coming from an environment of instability, Ayanna possessed a sixth sense for emotional shifts and inconsistencies. Something ailed Mustafa, and the text connected him to those issues.

Ayanna wanted him to know she understood. "Even without knowing what you said... the beauty of the recitation touched me."

"Dat's what da truth will do," Mustafa didn't want to spoil the moment with his thoughts.

Ayanna wanted to comfort him more. She had just shared an intimate moment with Mustafa. The details behind it were unclear. But Ayanna knew the glimmer of vulnerability she saw in Mustafa's eyes was rare. It expanded her comfort.

Ayanna took off her head wrap and let her locs down. They cascaded over her face. The look was mystical. Mustafa watched her, captivated. She pulled her hair back and Mustafa reached for her mane.

His hand rested on the nape of her neck and he pulled Ayanna to him. The kiss was deep. Their lips interlocked, causing the room to spin. Ayanna became flushed. She moaned and Mustafa slid his tongue into her mouth… just enough to delve right past her teeth… And then he pulled back.

Ayanna lost control. She crawled onto Mustafa's lap… grinded her pelvis into his groin. Mustafa's strong hand gathered and tugged her locs. His other hand slid down her spine, past the small of her back, and cupped her ass. His grip was firm and leading. They both found each other's rhythm and escaped into ecstasy.

They took the time to listen to each other. Every lick and pull. Each touch and kiss. All of their movements celebrated the other. And they prayed for it to not end.

The connection strengthened as the fire dwindled. And the joining of their spirits was more important than the details of their lovemaking. Sex became worship.

She needed him. And he needed her. And God had brought them together. They were thankful for it. The minutes turned into hours. And then they collapsed.

Their bodies drenched in sweat. Their privates swollen. Their muscles contracted. Tangled in each other's limps.

"The fire needs a few more logs," Mustafa whispered.

Her vagina tightened around his penis. She didn't want to disconnect.

"I think we are doing a good enough job at keeping each other warm," Ayanna reassured him.

Mustafa smiled. He kissed Ayanna on the forehead and peeled himself from beneath her. Ayanna moaned as he exited her body. She watched Mustafa walk to the fireplace. Her vagina throbbed… The yearning alerted Ayanna that she was letting her guard down too soon.

"So," Ayanna wondered how careful she should be with her words, "as your temporary wife, I would like to know what you do for a living."

Mustafa didn't turn around to face her. He stared deeper into the fire. He wasn't prepared for the question and his paranoia kicked in. "I told you… I hustle."

Ayanna heard the defensiveness in his tone. Her sentinels readied their arms. "Yeah… But what? I mean the average street nigga would give me the same answer if I asked them… nine times out of ten it's just code for selling dope."

"Then it's a good thang I ain't da average street nigga." Mustafa felt cornered.

"I wasn't saying you were… I'm just saying…."

"Look," Mustafa didn't want to go any further with the conversation, "I 'on't like to discuss my b'iness."

His tone was aggressive and it made Ayanna sit up. Her comfort was running away from her. Suddenly, even her nudity felt premature and out of place. She reached for her shirt and hurriedly put it on.

"Okay... So I guess the honeymoon is over." Ayanna welled up with fear; angry for allowing the fairytale to take shape in her mind. "Yasmeen was right... Ain't no telling what you're into... Talking 'bout you Muslim."

Ayanna had crossed the line. Mustafa sprung to his feet. "What is you sayin'?"

Ayanna- the rebel from Mississippi- wasn't one to back down from a fight. "I'm saying… What good is all this religion and rules if you are just like the rest of these niggas?"

Mustafa stood up. As he walked towards her, Ayanna could see the danger in his eyes. Apart of it intrigued her. "First off, I never said I did shit illegal. And me being born-n-raised Muslim don't change da fact dat I live in dis world. I do what I do ta survive. But I 'on't harm innocent people. Or terrorize my community, feel me."

Ayanna sensed Mustafa's words were true to him. But she still wanted more clarity, "So, what do you do?"

"Ayanna, I 'on't discuss my b'iness," his tone was matter of fact.

And Ayanna saw it wouldn't go any further. Something about Mustafa made her submit. "Okay... Well, I guess as the temporary wife, I only have certain rights, huh?"

Mustafa came and sat beside her. He touched her shoulder and rubbed his hands down her arm. He didn't want to be harsh. And he didn't want to push her away. But there were things about himself he couldn't reveal.

Ayanna wanted to be reluctant to his touch, but there was

something about Mustafa that drew her in. And the more she tried to pull away, the more she wanted to be closer to him. Their bond was real.

He took her chin in his hand and gently turned her face towards him. "Give us some time. Everythang will come to da light."

Ayanna stared into Mustafa's eyes. And once again the stranger became hauntingly familiar, and she allowed herself to believe what he said.

CHAPTER TWENTY-FIVE

Reek sat handcuffed in the interrogation room. The bracelets were tight and the more he moved the more the steel squeezed his wrist. He breathed. Chanted to himself.

The whole process was a mind game. Bright lights. White brick walls. A huge two-way mirror. Thermostat on low. All designed to create a feeling of being trapped. The procedure was designed to break a person's resolve; most people would tell on their grandmother to escape from an interrogation room.

Reek had been through the process so many times; he understood his getaway depended on him staying calm. Reek looked at the two-way mirror, and winked at whoever was observing him. He was built for the game.

On the other side of the glass Zimmer stood behind Officer Crawley. The Feds took a smoke break to discuss their strategy for interrogating Reek. Crawley had babysitting duty.

"He's not budging," Crawley informed Zimmer, "Frustrated the shit out of Agent Finn."

Zimmer snickered, "That's cause Feds don't talk local language."

Officer Crawly had been a uniformed officer for nearly 18 years. Although he never had the desire or the aptitude to make detective, he had mastered sensing ulterior motives. "What you need,

Detective?"

Zimmer loved how the old school detectives weren't too keen on small talk; so he shot straight from the hip, "Ten minutes. No camera."

Crawley smirked. He had seen the request coming from the moment Zimmer walked into the room. Crawley acted like he was mulling the idea over, but there was no question what side he buttered his bread. Rumors floated around the precinct about the Feds stepping on Zimmer's toes and back-seating him on his murder investigation. Crawley was from the old regime; no matter what, it was State versus Federal.

"Feds come in… keep my name out of it," Crawley laid his ground rule to cover his backside. He added, "Besides I love when the locals talk."

Zimmer slapped Crawley on the shoulder. He loved when an officer bled blue. They shared a smile. And as Zimmer rushed to the next room, Crawley cut off the cameras.

Reek heard the latch on the door. He prepared for another bout with the Feds. But when Zimmer walked through the door, he was thrown off.

Reek was familiar with the star detective. He had locked up a few of his homeboys over the years. But Zimmer was infamous for the Imam's arrest. Reek adjusted himself in his seat; the game had just gotten more intense.

Zimmer winked at Reek as he entered the room, with two thick files clutched in his paws. He sat down at the table and thumbed through Reek's jacket.

Without looking up, Zimmer began his manipulation, "You know what confuses the shit out of me? For a people that believe in a religion of sacrifice and discipline... y'all are worst than the common nigga."

Reek kept his poker face. A khafir's judgment didn't faze Reek, at all.

Zimmer was just getting started, "Tariq Mohammed... you've been busy over the years, huh?"

"Fuck ya want wit' me, man?" Reek wasn't in the mood for a slow fuck.

Zimmer loved to play hardball. "Fuck what I want wit' you... Feds got you boy. Undercover agent shot. You got his dope. Looks like the blood on your hands."

"Like I told da agent dat came in here already... I 'on't know shit about shit."

Zimmer smirked, went in his jacket, and like a magician pulled out the 9mm the Feds had recovered when they picked Reek up. He dropped it onto the desk. Zimmer had crept it from the observation room when he talked to Crawley.

"You don't know shit 'bout shit? You should put that on a t-shirt or something," Zimmer joked, "Cause something tells me when the forensics come back from this 9 the Feds found in your car you gonna know somethin'. Only thing is- by that time- it's gonna be too late for you. I can only imagine what the judge is gonna throw a terrorist for a quadruple homicide."

179

Reek tried to conceal his nervousness. Although, he had delivered none of the fatal shots on Holderness, his gun discharged. And like an idiot he held onto the weapon... despite Sal's instructions.

"I ain't do shit, bruh."

Zimmer sensed he had Reek on the ropes, "C'mon Mohammed... you can do better than that... You ever heard the old saying; my enemy's enemy is my friend... See, right now the Feds consider you and your crew public enemy number one."

Zimmer turned up the heat. He pulled out the photos of the dead bodies from Holderness, and laid them across the table. Zimmer stared at Reek the entire time. The two sat in silence. Reek found it was getting harder to maintain his disguise.

Zimmer continued, "They want you so bad that they don't give a fuck about these dead bodies... But I can't stand the fuckin' Feds. Which if the saying is right... that makes us friends."

Suddenly, Reek wanted to break free. He fidgeted in his seat. The handcuffs broke skin; Reek grimaced.

"Those bracelets too tight?" Zimmer was ready to move in for the kill, and even though, Reek didn't respond; Zimmer walked over and unlocked the cuffs. "I don't like my friends to be uncomfortable, Mohammed."

Reek massaged his wrist as he watched Zimmer retake his seat. There was more silence. Zimmer wanted Reek to have a second to think about the difference between having the cuffs off, or wearing them for the rest of his natural born life.

Zimmer proceeded, "So, let's talk... friend."

CHAPTER TWENTY-SIX

1.

Mustafa leapt onto Saif's front porch. Even though the hellhounds were still on his heels, Mustafa's night in the mountains left him invigorated. And Mustafa had faith he'd find his way out of his current situation. He remembered Allah wouldn't put anything on him that he didn't have the strength to bare.

Mustafa knocked on Saif's front door. While he waited for someone to answer, he checked his surroundings. Saif's son, Jabril, answered the door. Mustafa loved Saif's kids. And he loved how his brother took care of his family. Mustafa wanted that love and stability in is life. And he wanted to fulfill the other half of his faith.

Mustafa knelt down and smiled, "Slaama-Laikum, lil souljah."

"Uncle Mustafa, you know I can beat up my daddy now," Jabril was always excited to see his Uncle Mustafa. He wanted to show Mustafa he was indeed a soldier.

"What? You don't return the greetin'?" Mustafa gently scolded.

"Oh. Slaama-Laikum, Uncle Mustafa," Jabril had other things on his mind, "you know I can beat up my daddy now?"

"I 'on't know 'bout dat... Your Abu is a pretty tough guy."

"Yes, huh... I'm tough too," Jabril put up his fist.

Mustafa admired Jabril's fire, "C'mon, what ya got?"

"Jabril," Khadijah fussed as she stormed into the room, "didn't nobody tell you to open that door."

Jabril got caught red-handed, but like his father he wasn't going down without a fight, "It was just Uncle Mustafa, Ummi."

Khadijah clenched her teeth together, "Boy if you don't get your tail…" Before she finished her sentence Khadijah reached for Jabril, but he was too quick. Khadijah couldn't get to him fast enough. Mustafa laughed as Jabril shook his mother.

Khadijah rolled her eyes; she was defeated. "Gonna drive me crazy, Mustafa."

"Al-Hamdulillah," Mustafa smiled. They both recognized the blessing.

"Let me go get, Saifullah. He's back in the studio." Even though Khadijah had known Mustafa all of her life, as a married woman she didn't linger around other men.

"The studio?" The news surprised Mustafa.

Once upon a time, Saif's alter-ego, Lion, was going to be Saifullah's way out of the streets. And he was talented. Then Khadijah became pregnant, and they got married. With a wife and a child on the way, Saif's talent became a mere pipe dream… A hobby he rarely indulged in.

"I know, right," Khadijah was excited too. She loved when Saif was home, and she adored it when her husband did something that made him happy. "Been in there all night," Khadijah's eyes lit up.

"My ears were burning."

Neither Khadijah nor Mustafa saw Saif walk up.

"Your earphones were probably too loud," Khadijah teased.

They shared a quick peck on the lips. As Mustafa watched the happily married couple, he thought of Ayanna.

Khadijah walked to the back. Saif watched her leave. And once she was out of sight his demeanor became serious.

"Slaama-Laikum," Saif reached his hand out to Mustafa.

"Laikum-Salaam."

Saif took a moment to size his partner up. "Let's take a walk."

The two exited the house. They both checked their surroundings; looked around to see who could be watching them. War was stressful. Saif took out a fresh pack of cigarettes and packed them in his palm. Mustafa became a little concerned since cigarettes were another one of Saif's old habits he rarely indulged in.

"So, you in the studio?" Mustafa decided to address the least controversial surprise first.

"Yeah," Saif lit his cigarette, "Just tryna find some peace... since I couldn't find you."

Saif's emotional reaction set off alarms in Mustafa's head. It was out of character for Saif. "I told you what was up.... What's really good whichu?" Mustafa responded.

Saif looked off and then back at Mustafa, "You heard from Reek?"

"Naw."

Saif wanted to say, *how could you, nigga, you ain't answered your phone.* But he tamed his tongue, "Ya boi got picked up by dem people yesterday?"

"Man, hell naw... For what?" Mustafa had a guess.

"I can tell you what I think... But I 'on't know, for real-for real. But it was dem Feds. All da Alphabets... thang is... he already out."

"Get da fuck outta here... Dat nigga a knucklehead... he gotta sheet."

"Exactly... nigga on paper," Saif reminded Mustafa, "and he ain't call nobody... And den, poof, ya out. Shittin' me, homes."

Mustafa's mind did cartwheels. *What the fuck did Reek do? What did he say to get free?* Mustafa had let his guard down. Mustafa believed life was a series of decisions. And his choice to let Reek hold the work was a stupid one. The walls closed around him.

"Aye yo... I'm gonna get up outta here."

"Aight," Saif wanted more information. "So, what you thinking?"

"I 'on't know what ta think," Mustafa needed to be transparent. "Let's meet over dere at Bruh's spot tonight. Don't say shit 'bout shit, and we'll know exactly what it is."

2.

Brother Abdullah stood outside his restaurant and talked philosophy with an older akh. Mustafa careened his SUV into the parking space. Abdullah wrapped up the conversation and was there to greet Mustafa as he exited his automobile. Mustafa and Brother Abdullah embraced cheek to cheek, three times.

"Slaama-Laikum"

"Wa-Alaikum- As-Salaam-wa-Barakhatuhu," Bro Abdullah

returned the greeting. "You good son?"

"I 'on't know," Mustafa confessed, "Thangs ain't all da way in control."

"I heard," Abdullah lowered his voice, "Heard it on tha scanners first. And then tha rumor mill say he already out."

"On some next day shit," Mustafa seldom cursed when addressing Brother Abdullah.

"You know it ain't no way, right?" Brother Abdullah intended for the question to be rhetorical. "What he say?"

"Ain't talked to him yet."

"Don't matter what come' out his mouth," Brother Abdullah stated. "The question is what you gonna do?"

"Dat's what I'm tryna figure out."

Abdullah understood the hard decision. Battle was full of rough choices. It's what separated the soldiers from the civilians. So, Bro Abdullah reminded Mustafa of his duty, "I know, you don't need no mo' bodies... But you can't have half-truth around you. I know y'all got history, but there can't be no weak links on the frontline, Mustafa."

Mustafa just nodded his head and watched the traffic go by. "Ya right," he conceded.

"So, you want to put us on pause?" Brother Abdullah's mind was always on his money.

"Ain't no need," Mustafa had the same train of thought, "Saif the only one I told so far."

"And then what?"

"I 'on't know... Retirement lookin' good," Mustafa joked, and then realized the statement was damn near prophetic. "Jus' don't need ta be forced into it."

"Insha-Allah," Brother Abdullah had been around long enough to understand it could go either way.

"Insha-Allah." Mustafa echoed.

3.

Bro Abdullah responded just as Mustafa expected. The answer was clear. He drove around for a few hours... Cruised on familiar streets and gave his mind a chance to rest.

Mustafa didn't want to kill another Muslim. He had long made peace with the fact that sometimes he had to take a disbelievers head. But Reek was close to Mustafa; he was crew. And unlike Reek, Mustafa's loyalty was limitless.

The sun descended behind the towers in Atlanta's skyline. And the colors of dusk reminded Mustafa it was time for one of his favorite prayers. Maghrib. The evening salat.

Mustafa was always happy to pray with other believers. It was one thing to visualize millions of Muslims standing with him in unison. But it was a different beast for Mustafa to look to his left and right, and his akhs were flanked shoulder to shoulder and toe to toe. Brothers, who followed his philosophies. Comrades, who would fight in defense of his faith. Muslims. To Mustafa there was no deeper bond.

Mustafa exited the masjid. The prayer didn't ease his heavy

heart.

"As-Salaamu-Alaikum! Mustafa! Hold up a second!"

Mustafa looked over his shoulder and spotted Imam Farooq. It never ceased to amaze Mustafa how smaller in stature Imam Farooq was than Imam Yusuf; short and chubby with dark skin. He actually looked like the Imam's opposite. Mustafa reluctantly exchanged Salaams and the customary cheek-to-cheek embrace.

"I've been trying to catch up with you," Imam Farooq stated.

"Oh yeah?"

"Yeah," Imam Farooq took his time, "Look, I know there's a lot going on in the neighborhood right now…"

"Mashallah," Mustafa cut him off at path, "I cain't help you wit' dat."

"Mashallah," Imam Farooq was prepared for the conversation, "But I think you can, akhi. See, I know that you have a lot of influence with the young brothers in the Ummah, and that y'all grew up under Imam Yusuf… And I know some people in the congregation are feeling like I am just the temporary Imam or that I don't…"

Imam Farooq watched his steps. "Look, akh, Allah is the best of planners. And I have a great deal of respect for the Imam. But I can't say I was fond of all of his methods."

"Methods?" Mustafa checked his temper. Imam Farooq was lucky Mustafa had just made prayer. "I 'on't know what ya talmbout Imam Farooq. And wit' all due respect Imam Yusuf gonna always be my Imam… ya dig?"

A moment of silence gave each man the time to decide his next move.

"Yeah I dig," Imam Farooq moved first, "But I also dig that nothing stays the same. And as a believer we have to have faith in Allah's change. Allah is change, Mustafa. And surely, everything done in the dark will be brought to light."

Mustafa didn't know if he was being taught or warned. But he didn't want to add Imam Farooq's little soliloquy to his plate. Mustafa thought muteness would be a better play.

"Yeah... aight. Well, if dat's all," Mustafa's glare made sure it would be. "I gotta get outta here. Slamma-Laikum."

Imam Farooq nodded. He was aware of Mustafa's reputation and got exactly what he thought he would. "Wa-Alaikum-As-Salaam-wa-Rahmatullah-wa-Barakhatuhu... Mustafa."

Imam Farooq's greeting resonated with Mustafa. It loitered in his mind. He wished Imam Farooq had not disturbed his thoughts. The unwarranted clamor was a distraction, and he couldn't afford any missteps.

4.

The after-hours spot was in the West End. Folded beneath MARTA's elevated train tracks, hidden in plain sight. It was the perfect place for a murder.

Imam Farooq's statement still sounded in Mustafa's head. He fingered his dhikr beads and concentrated on what was before him. Everybody was in position for Reek's surprise party.

Saif's eyes were bloodshot and darted back and forth to the door. He chain-smoked cigarettes and shared a bottle of Crown with Bruh, one of their childhood friends. Bruh was part of a group of Muslims that where sent to live in Senegal for their teenage years because the Dunya had begun to take hold of them.

The relocation was supposed to save the young men from themselves. But most times the young warriors returned with more fire than they left with. Bruh was a killer… something he brought back with him from the bush. Bruh wore the years of street life and chain gangs on his face and in his shoulders. He drug the souls of bodies he had buried in his eyes.

The tension in the room was thick.

But Reek paid it no attention when he bopped into the spot. "Slaama-Laikum!"

Reek dapped everybody, seeming to not notice the half-hearted returns his greetings received.

"What it is Bruh?" Reek shouted out.

Reek and Bruh were as thick as thieves. They shared the trait of a shaky morality and supported each other's schemes. Bruh was going to hate to see Reek go, but he hated a snitch.

"Just tryna keep the grass cut." Bruh didn't bullshit.

"No doubt." Reek walked behind the bar, as it was normal for him to do so, and poured a shot.

Bruh looked at Mustafa… Mustafa nodded. And Bruh went to lock the door. Oblivious to the movement, Reek came from behind the bar and walked toward Mustafa.

"So, what da deal?" Reek took his shot. "We got some work or somethin'?"

"I should be askin' you dat question?" Mustafa replied.

Bruh reappeared.

Saif got off of his stool and flanked Reek's other side.

Reek finally tuned in to the climate of the room.

Once he adjusted to the temperature, he believed he had to play it ice-cold, "What ya talmbout, akhi?"

Mustafa smirked and wrapped his beads around his wrist. He moved in closer. "Ya hear ya guy?"

Saif snickered... But his eyes didn't reflect his smile.

Reek quickly turned to Saif, "What goin' on, Saif?

Reek waited for a response. And Mustafa slipped the pistol out of his waistband, grabbed Reek around the collar, and slapped him across the temple with the gun.

"Fuck!" The steel opened Reek's face; he leaked.

Bruh rushed over and grabbed Reek's pistol before he could get to it.

"What I'm talmbout?" Mustafa hit him again. The metal cracked against Reek's skull. "Same thang everybody else is talmbout, nigga!"

"What da fuck, Stafa?"

Mustafa faked like he was going to hit Reek again. Reek flinched in Mustafa's clutch. And Mustafa turned the muzzle to Reek's face. Reek became faint.

"What you tell da police?"

"I 'on't know what you are talmbout, akh!"

Mustafa hit Reek with the butt of the gun and pulled the trigger at the same time. The heat from the gun blast stung Reek's face. His ears rang. And even though he wasn't shot, he was so discombobulated he wasn't sure if the blood was from his spanking or if Mustafa had sent a bullet through his head.

"Wallahee, Tariq... I will open up your head if you keep playin' wit' me!"

"I ain't say shit, akh!" Reek plead for his life, "C'mon Mustafa you know me... I'm a lot of things but I ain't no fuckin snitch."

"So, why dem people let you out?"

"It was jus' a quarter key of dope."

Mustafa hit him again. "Who da fuck you think you talkin' to... Dem people 'on't show up for dat type shit."

Reek fell to his knees, "Wallahee, Mustafa! I ain't tell dem people shit... I know... I know... I ain't say shit 'bout getting knocked, but we ain't been a hun'red and I ain't want ya ta know I been servin'."

"Where'd you get the dope?"

"What you talmbout?"

Mustafa hit him again.

"Fuck! Okay... Aight... It was from the lick on Holderness. I fucked up, man. I needed dat bread... But I ain't say shit... I ain't tell dem people nuthin'."

Mustafa dug the muzzle into Reek's jaw, "You a fuckin' liar."

"I know... I am. But I ain't tell 'em shit. Wallahee!"

Mustafa tensed his grip on the pistol.

Reek was near tears, "Wallahee, akh... Wallahee."

Mustafa tossed Reek to the side. Reek stammered to his feet, held his head, and looked to Saif and Bruh. They glared back. Reek thought the chance of him making it out the club alive was slim to none... Even if it wasn't Mustafa who pulled the trigger.

"You done ova here," Mustafa announced, "West End ain't your home no mo'. You 'on't get no money over here. It ain't where you worship. Or where you turn your hoes into housewives. B'lieve dat dis my only time showin' you mercy. Wallahee! Get da fuck outta here!"

Reek paused he couldn't believe Mustafa was going to let him leave.

"Oh, hell naw!" Saif couldn't accept it either. Saif moved towards Reek. Reek back peddled. Bruh snuck up and stood in Reek's path. And then Mustafa stopped Saif cold; he laid the pistol flat onto Saif's chest.

"You got other work to do," Mustafa looked at Bruh, "Let him go."

Not used to following orders, it took a moment before Bruh cleared Reek's path. Saif fumed.

"I called the play." Mustafa announced.

Mustafa turned his back, and Reek scurried out the door. Mustafa staggered to one of the couches, unraveled his dhikr beads, and began to chant: *ir-Rahim*... His Lord was Merciful. Mercy was the Sunnah of the Prophet. Although it was not the practice of the streets, Mustafa needed to follow a more honorable path.

CHAPTER TWENTY-SEVEN

1.

Mustafa barely slept. By the time he had closed his eyes, the first slither of light broke the darkness. *Fajr.* The Dawn.

After Mustafa made his prayer, he went and sat on the park bench to watch the sun rise. The morning dew and the fog seemed to teeter on the lines of surreal. Mustafa's had turned into a walking nightmare. And the mystic morning fell right in line.

"You up early." Saif appeared like a ghost.

"Fajr."

"Yeah," Saif could relate.

Saif sat, on the back of the park bench, next to Mustafa. He took a moment to take in the spiritual feel of the dawn. But got down to business.

"Wha' goin' on wit' you, akh?" Saif studied his brother's face. "Ya know dat nigga talkin'- don't you?"

"I 'on't know what he said. But I know I'm tired. And what's another dead body gonna do, Saif... If dese people comin' dey comin'. I'd rather shoot it out wit' dem, dan kill one of my own."

Saif wiped his hands over his face. He had already made another decision, "Stafa, you my guy for as long as I can remember. We hunt and gather together, homes, and I respect how ya mind work, real talk. But I cain't jeopardize my family behind dat nigga Reek or whateva it is ya got goin' on. Dere's rules to dis game for a reason, akh."

Mustafa didn't have an argument. He broke the code by letting Reek escape. Mustafa had chosen his life. And Mustafa understood that when his hands testified for him on Judgment Day, they would have to admit to dirt he did... But Mustafa didn't want to paint them with the blood of a Muslim.

But Mustafa was responsible for more than himself. He didn't want to break the trust between him and Saif. Mustafa stated his position, but he understood he had a job to do.

"I got you," Mustafa said regretfully.

Saif appreciated that Mustafa was willing to step-up, but he couldn't take any chances. "You want me to handle this?"

"Naw, I got it... I brought Reek in."

"Yeah..." Saif didn't want to play the blame game.

"Plus," Mustafa was still calling the shots, "you got your hands full wit' your friend."

Saif spat and watched the phlegm catch a blade of grass. He was more than pleased to carry out his duty. "Dat's light work. But Reek ain't gonna be as easy... 'specially after he done slivered away."

Mustafa recognized finding Reek could pose a problem. "I'll turn over da rocks and find out where he hidin'. I'll hit you up, if I need you. We got a driver for tomorrow?"

"Yeah, I got it covered... I'll make sure he A-1."

That was the only explanation Mustafa needed.

They both stood up.

"We just gotta get dis straight and den you can rest," there was no sarcasm in Saif's voice. He wished peace for Mustafa because he wanted for his brother what he wanted for himself.

Mustafa felt it was sincere and extended his hand, "Slaama-Laikum."

Saif's embrace was tight, "Laikum-Salaam."

And the two friends left in opposite directions- leaving an empty park bench.

2.

Mustafa went home and rested his mind before starting his manhunt for Reek. His first stop was Rashida's house. Reek was a creature of habit. So, when Mustafa knocked on Rashida's front door, he was sure Reek was on the other side.

As Mustafa waited he turned toward the street. He saw a strange white van, with no windows, parked at the curb. Mustafa's paranoia aligned with his instinct. He decided even if Reek were inside, he would have to find another place to carry out his execution.

Rashida jerked the door open and everything moved and shook just like it was supposed to. She wore a wife beater, no bra, and some boy shorts. Her nipples protruded through the ribs in the preshrunk cotton tee.

Mustafa tried to lower his gaze, but ended up counting the cascade of stars that was inked down her thigh. She was perfectly shaped; her flesh had the perfect mix of soft and firm.

"Oh, hey, Mustafa." Her chest poked out; her legs cocked apart.

"Slaama-Laikum." Regardless Mustafa maintained respect.

"Mmm... what up?" She wanted him to no she wasn't *fucking with that campaign.*

Mustafa got down to business, "I'm lookin' for Reek."

"I ain't seen dat nigga... wa'n't my turn... I been alone... all night long," she took a deep breath and opened the door a little wider, "you wanna come in?"

"Naw," Mustafa looked over her shoulder, "jus' tell 'im I came by. I need to talk to 'im. Tell 'im it was a misunderstandin'... we good."

"Okay... whateva you need, Stafa," the statement sounded lewd.

Mustafa didn't see a need to end with the greeting. Rashida smirked as Mustafa walked away... It tickled her that Mustafa played the role of disciplined believer. He was a gangster. And Rashida was sure of it from the fresh moisture between her thighs.

Rashida snickered as she switched her tail to the couch. She flopped down and opened a magazine. She flipped through the pages and popped her gum; the entire interaction pleased her. She enjoyed exposing her body to Mustafa. She adored the thought of Mustafa finding it difficult to resist her advances.

"Fuckin' stupid ass... what if he woulda came in?"

And she loved that Reek hid in the shadows... it emasculated him and she got to take part.

"Mustafa' self righteous ass wa'n't comin' 'cross dat doorway... dat's why I went like dis in da first place," she told part of the truth.

It turned her on to push up on the boss.

"Whateva," Reek wanted to lash out, "Da fuck I fuck wit' yo' ratchet ass fo'?"

"Jus' 'cause dese niggas got you in hidin'- don't start wit' me," Rashida had no respect for a coward, "I ain't got nuthin to do wit' you gettin' fucked up."

Reek walked over to Rashida… his face was lumped and gashed up. Rashida stared at him. She wanted to laugh as he paced back and forth. *Your scary ass*, she thought.

"What da fuck do he want?" Reek felt trapped, again. He had escaped death the other night, and Mustafa came back to collect. "I gotta do somethin'."

Reek reached in his pocket and pulled out a business card. Reek stared at the phone. He had to find his way out.

3.

Meanwhile, in his downtown office Levison brokered for his own future. He hadn't talked to Mustafa, since their last meeting. Levison needed to ensure the Feds handled their end of the bargain before Mustafa started along his warpath.

"We have to be on top of this Councilman… Okay, well let me get out of here… we'll talk, my friend. Okay." Levison wiped his hands over his face… Leaving the safety of his office had become the most stressful part of his day.

Levison poured himself a shot, opened a pill bottle, and washed down the Percosets with hard liquor. Prescription pill cocktails helped him cope with his greed.

Levison wanted in on the ground floor of the Westside's gentrification. And the Feds told him they built a case that would link Mustafa to Imam Yusuf. And then they could fabricate a criminal enterprise. Levison didn't care about the politics.

But his gluttony blinded him. Mustafa wasn't a simpleton. Levison realized he had opened a can of cobras. And they had to be captured before they struck.

Levison floated off the elevator and into the parking garage. The dope had him seeing everything in a haze. He adjusted his eyes to the darkness.

Then, in the emptiness Levison heard a sound echo in the garage. The cement walls bounced the sound around, and Levison couldn't pinpoint its origin. He strained his eyes and tried to bring everything in focus.

And then he heard it again. His head swiveled as the noise ricocheted through the cement tomb. But he saw nothing. Levison walked faster through the dark deck. Just as he hit the car alarm and reached for the door handle...

"What up, my friend," an unfriendly voice called out.

Levison turned around and saw Saif- a black and white checkered scarf draped over his head. He hid in the shadows. The grim reaper.

Levison squinted his dilated pupils. The drugs mixed with terror, and Levison knees buckled. His grip on the door kept him from falling. "Saifullah? What's going on?"

"Dere you go wit' dat full name shit."

Saif walked out of the dark and brought himself into clear view. He wanted Levison to see the whites of his eyes.

Levison scrambled. "Hey... I'm... I'm just on my way home," he stuttered. Levison grabbed at the handle and it slipped out of his grip. "Is there something I can do for you?"

Saif looked around and made sure it was just the two of them. "Yeah, Mustafa wanted me ta give ya somethin'."

Levison settled. Maybe he had given Mustafa too much credit. If Mustafa still wanted to do business, then money blinded him like it did every other 'hood nigga.

"Did he send the jewels?" Levison was eager to pocket the jewels off the record. "I mean- because I didn't know what all that was about the other day."

"Naw... its betta dan jewels." Saif was less than a foot from Levison.

Levison figured if he wasn't already shot, then Saif was definitely there to negotiate. "Better than jewels? And what's that?"

"A trip to ya maker." Saif raised the machete he had tucked to his side. And with an effortless motion he drew the blade across Levison's throat. The sharp piece of steel opened Levison's esophagus, and the blood pumped out the wide gash. Levison reached for his own neck... he hoped he could stop the bleeding.... Or stop his head from his falling off his shoulder.

But Saif was swift. He jammed the blade into Levison's chest plate. It broke through the bone and stabbed into Levison's heart.

"Bismillah," Saif leaned in close and whispered. It was the last words the Jewish man heard as he slipped into darkness. "You gonna need that, my friend."

Saif believed his actions were righteous… And that Levison had a place in hell.

CHAPTER TWENTY-EIGHT

1.

As the sun made its way to the top of the morning sky, Ayanna- on her hands and knees- turned the soil. She hadn't heard from Mustafa since their return from their temporary honeymoon. Even though forty-eight hours had barely passed, she wondered if Mustafa had lured her into a spiritual one nightstand.

Yasmeen stood over her. Yani called on Yasmeen when she needed to shut down her sensitivities. Yasmeen only dealt with the bottom line.

"Oh, it's definitely illegal. Unless it's some extra broke shit." Yasmeen had dated her fair share of criminals... and bums.

"Naw, his pockets are straight. I don't think he could even be broke," Ayanna reflected on Mustafa's apparent strength, "Don't seem like his nature."

"Then it's illegal. College niggas and corporate squares love to brag. They act like they're some sort of commodity." Yasmeen waved off an insect. "I don't know... maybe he just needs that better half to help him see the error of his ways."

Ayanna darted her eyes at Yasmeen.

"What?" Yasmeen feigned insulted. "I ain't wit' true love with those broke-ass stray revolutionaries you rescue at your rallies."

Ayanna rolled her eyes, "You a trip."

"I'm saying- fine and successful. Some of these niggas just get some bad cards. And if he smart enough to hold his hand... I'll show him how he should play 'em... Try meeting him on his terms."

Ayanna looked around like she was in the twilight zone. "Who tha fuck are you?"

Yasmeen waved off another insect; she didn't need to defend her position. "Hopefully, he can get you to come indoors."

Ayanna wanted to laugh but instead she shook her head and continued to dig.

2.

As the sun disappeared into the edge of the Earth; Ayanna lit candles, poured a large glass of wine, rolled a joint, and decided she would occupy her mind with work. She took extra-time with each pair of earrings; it was her way of ruling the silence. Every time Mustafa crept into her thoughts she washed him away with a gulp of wine.

And right before midnight, as Ayanna's eyes started to close, her doorbell rang.

Ayanna sat up. A rush of confusion and excitement ran towards her. The doorbell rang again. She took another swallow from her glass and raced to the peephole. In her fisheye view, Mustafa stared back at her.

Ayanna collapsed off her tiptoes and thought about Mustafa's sudden arrival. *Why didn't he call?* She checked her appearance in the mirror and took three deep breaths.

The doorbell rang again.

"One moment, please." Ayanna finished her wine, placed it on the foyer table, and cracked her front door.

"Hey." She didn't want to sound too welcoming or too defensive. "What are you doing here?"

Mustafa opened with a joke, "I guess the honeymoon is over."

"I didn't mean it like that." The longer Mustafa stood in her doorway, the quicker Ayanna realized she was happy to see him. "I just wasn't expecting you."

"I didn't expect to come over, to be honest." Mustafa hoped she didn't read his statement wrong. "I looked up and the next thing I know I was ringing the bell."

Ayanna wasn't sure how to receive it, but she was willing to figure it out. "You want to come in."

Mustafa thought it would be best to give his tongue a rest; he nodded and made his way over the threshold. Ayanna closed the door behind him and paused. Mustafa soaked in her apartment. It was exactly what he expected it to be.

"So," Ayanna grabbed at his attention, "What's up?"

"Yeah... So..." Mustafa didn't want to stop taking in the peace. He looked in Ayanna's eyes and sensed he was running out of time. "I'm getting out of town for a minute."

"Really... Where are you going?"

Mustafa looked at the floor...

"Top secret?" Ayanna jabbed.

"Naw... I don't really know where I'm going."

"Sounds interesting." *Or illegal*, Ayanna thought. She wanted to connect with Mustafa, but the guards were at their posts. "So, I guess we are officially separated then."

"Well actually," Mustafa believed the spoils favored the bold. "I was wondering what do you have going on?"

She decided that her first line of defense would be to ask for clarity, "What do you mean?"

"I mean," Mustafa was usually more direct with his words, "The marriage doesn't have to end."

Ayanna's heart skipped. "Mustafa, are you asking me to leave with you?"

"Yep... I am."

Ayanna ignored the resurgence of her fantasy and listened to Mustafa's question in more practical terms. Mustafa was a stranger, she reminded herself. And Yasmeen confirmed her suspicion about Mustafa's illicit lifestyle. She thanked The Most High for insight. Left to her own devices, Ayanna would have jumped onto the back of Mustafa's stead and galloped off into the sunset.

"Mustafa, I think you're a wonderful man," she wanted to be gentle. "I mean, going up to the mountains was one thing but I don't know you well enough to run away with you..."

"What do you need to know?"

"What you do for a living, for one?"

Mustafa looked away. He wished he could tell Ayanna more about his life. He needed somewhere to lay his burdens... someone to confide in. Instead, her merited inquiry made him isolate further.

His silence frustrated Ayanna. "Let's try something easier then... like... where are you going? Or how about why are you leaving in the first place?"

Mustafa realized he didn't think his request through, which was totally out of character. He wished he could save face and pull back his question. Time only moved forward, though.

"Ya right... I... I'm jus' at dat place... Ya know..." Mustafa's soul wanted to be more visible. "It's like da thangs dat I' been doin' fo'eva don't make da same sense dat dey used to."

Ayanna saw the vulnerability in his eyes again. She remembered their night in the mountains. And her natural inclination caused her to reach out to him. She touched his face, "Yeah... I know that place."

Mustafa leaned into her touch and mumbled to himself, "I'm at peace wit' you." And as he heard the words become audible, he realized that he was loosing control. He grabbed Ayanna's hand. "But you right- it was selfish of me ta pop up here like dis... askin' you what I'm askin'."

"It's all good." Ayanna didn't want to disconnect.

The two stared at each other for a moment. Mustafa pulled Ayanna in for a hug. Ayanna melted in his arms. They found peace in each other's embrace.

"Aight, Farmer Yani. Be good," Mustafa whispered without letting her go.

She didn't answer. Ayanna wanted to say; *fine I'll leave with you...*

it doesn't matter who you are or why you're leaving. But instead she just let out a moan.

Mustafa unwrapped Ayanna and kissed her on the forehead.

She remained quiet- too frightened to speak.

And as Mustafa hit an about-face, she came up with a way to extend the moment, "You know... Whatever you're dealing with, is still gonna be there tomorrow."

Mustafa was happy that it wasn't goodbye.

"Why don't you stay with me tonight?" Ayanna proposed. "Rest your head. Lick your wounds. Would you like that?"

Once again, Mustafa thought that his smartest response would be a head nod.

They laid together in silence that night. Mustafa didn't try to make love to her, which came of no surprise to Ayanna.

He placed his solid body against Ayanna's and rested his head on her chest. Before she knew it, Mustafa's breathing slowed down and he fell deep into slumber. Ayanna followed him into his dreams.

She didn't feel Mustafa slip from her arms. But when she opened her eyes he was gone. She felt her heart sink. Ayanna had literally met the man of her dreams and he had disappeared from her life as quickly as he appeared.

She walked to the window; the night sky was empty excepted for the narrow light of the crescent moon and the bright star that seemed to rest in its cradle. She closed her eyes and prayed for peace in Mustafa's journey.

CHAPTER TWENTY-NINE

1.

"Our Lord! Forgive us our sins and our transgressions, establish our feet firmly, and give us victory over the disbelieving folk," the Arabic echoed in the empty room.

Mustafa sat on the floor at the foot of his prayer rug. He had to get his mind ready for the lick... and he couldn't get prepared waking up on Ayanna's bosom. He hated to leave without saying goodbye. But if he didn't slip away he would have stayed in her arms forever.

Ayanna challenged his beliefs; made Mustafa look at his actions. Even as he stood at the counter and loaded his weaponry, he's routine felt abnormal. There was heaviness to his task. He cocked his .45 and put it on his hip. It was the first time the gun didn't feel like a natural extension of his body.

What good is all the discipline and sacrifice if you are just like the rest of theses niggas? Ayanna's question had infiltrated Mustafa's mind, and he no longer heard Ayanna's voice. The analysis had become his own. He shoved his sawed-off in the bag and tried to silence the voices in his head.

As he walked to the van, Mustafa had a sudden urge to call off the job. But it wasn't an option. His choices backed him into a corner and there was no place to run; he had to fight his way out.

Just as Mustafa reached the van, a police car appeared. The

officer and Mustafa locked eyes. The officer nodded, and Mustafa watched him pass. A quiet voice in the back of Mustafa's mind thought the officer was a validation of his reluctance. But he pushed on.

Mustafa jumped in the work-van. He checked the side mirror to make sure the pig didn't hit a U-turn.

"Khafir," Mustafa mumbled under his breath.

Mustafa looked over to the driver's seat. He had no idea who was behind the wheel... But Mustafa saw a familiar face...

Shim didn't initially see his brother's pearly whites; he was too busy making sure the overseer was out of the picture as well. Shim turned from the rearview. And Mustafa's rare smile became an image he would hold onto for the rest of his life.

Shim smiled back, "Ya thought I was gonna stay tucked down dere forever?"

"Naw," Mustafa closed down his smile, "Cain't stop a souljah." He playfully jabbed at Shim's body, "You good? You ready?"

Shim straightened his face and looked Mustafa squarely in his eyes, "I got ya, akh."

Mustafa glared back at Shim. Mustafa nodded, "Let's go get dis money, den."

"Leh go" Saif declared from the backseat. Although Reek was still on the loose, his absence from the job gave Saif peace. He trusted Mustafa and Shim. *A-1 Day-1's*. He would die for them, and they would do the same.

2.

The van pulled up in front of the store. Mustafa and Saif draped their keffiyehs over their heads. Shim put his gun on his lap and checked his mirrors. The streets were empty.

"We should be in and out. My people say nobody should even be close to here for a few hours." Mustafa prayed the information was correct.

"Ain't nuthin', akh," Shim reassured Mustafa.

Mustafa and Saif checked their surroundings and exited the car. They stared in each other's eyes and nodded. Saif entered first and Mustafa looked at his watch.

Inside the store, Saif bee-lined to the drink cooler. The Old Man observed Saif's every movement. Saif rapped out loud as he bopped down the aisle. He feigned confusion on his drink selection and used the reflection of the cooler doors to make sure it was just him and The Old Man. Saif slammed the cooler door, and mobbed towards the front of the store.

Just as Saif reached the counter, Mustafa walked in… He kept the door open and acted like he was looking for somebody. The Old Man eyed Mustafa.

"Aye man," Saif snapped. "Lemme get a pack of dem cigars back there! I gotta catch dis bus, shawdy!"

The Old Man looked at Saif and left Mustafa unsupervised.

"What kind?" The Old Man matched Saif's aggression.

"Those blue ones back there," Saif barked.

The Old Man's attention then went to the shelf behind him.

And Saif slid the two Desert Eagles from the small of his back. Mustafa locked the door...

The Old Man took his time and finally grabbed a green pack of cigars... something he was famous for doing.

"Hell naw... Not dem! Dat's fuckin' green," Saif became livid, "You 'on't know your colors... What da fuck man!"

The Old Man turned back and tried to find a blue pack. But there wasn't one.

"No blue pack, man."

He threw his hands up in desperation. He rotated back to the counter. And Saif shoved the two canons into The Old Man's face. "Jus' gimme da god damn green ones!"

Mustafa darted behind the counter. Under normal circumstances the plexi-glass would have been pulled closed, and the door locked. But it was Sunday morning and all the heathens were supposed to be sleep.

Outside the store Shim kept his head on a swivel. And then in his rearview a white Crown Victoria turned onto Ralph David. Shim peeped the black spotlight attached to the driver's side window pain. His tightened his grip on his .44 Mag...

The Crown Vic drove pass. The driver looked over at Shim and mashed the gas.

"Damn, police car," Shim snarled. He hated the Crown Vics bought at government auctions. The vehicles subconsciously created more police presence.

The converted squad car distracted Shim. And the young lady

pushing the baby stroller surprised him when she popped into Shim's peripheral. He turned his head and the white spandexes caught his attention. He watched the young lady switch her tale to the corner. She came to a stop and bent over to get a bag of chips for the toddler in the stroller.

"Mashallah," Shim muttered.

Shim shook her from his eyes. He reached to adjust his rearview mirror. The sudden movement sent a pain through his shoulder. Shim pulled his arm into the pain, and rotated the limb. He closed his eyes to cope with the throbbing.

And when he opened them, a van emerged in his rearview. Shim figured it was about a quarter-mile behind him. He adjusted in his seat. Shim couldn't see the driver, but he sensed something was wrong.

Shim wasn't the only person to take notice of the inconsistency. In the approaching van, Blacka and Copper saw the strange vehicle parked in front of their pickup location.

"Wah dat up dere," Copper asked as he turned down the music.

Blacka strained his eyes and reached for his Tech-9.

The van closed in, and the crowns of dreadlocks became visible. Shim darted his eyes toward the store. And then the van was behind him.

"Fuck..." Shim muttered.

Blacka had the same reaction, "Who da fuck, mi son?"

Copper cocked his Glock 40.

Neither van made an immediate move...

Across the street the toddler screamed for her chips. Shim looked over; her fine ass momma munched on the snack and gossiped on her cell phone. Shim glanced back to the Jamaicans... and then back at the store.

Suddenly, Mustafa's back appeared against the plexi-glass door. Shim said a dua and reached for his latch.

Mustafa stepped out the front door and Blacka spotted him. "Fuckin' Bumbaclad!"

The Jamaicans scrambled out the van. Shim was already ahead of them. Shim bust at Blacka, and the dread ducked behind the driver's side door.

The shot shocked Mustafa. He pivoted toward the Jamaicans. And fired a missile at Copper.

The blast tore into the passenger side door and shattered out the window.

Shim held Blacka in position with three shots to Blacka's shield. Blacka, stooped behind his door, extended his arm through the broken window, and blasted toward Shim.

Copper jumped from his cover and fired at Mustafa. The slug caught Mustafa in the shoulder. He was jerked off his feet, hit the ground, and scrambled to the front of the van. Shim watched the hit in slow motion. He loved Mustafa. The tears formed in his eyes as he hurled hot rocks at Copper. The bullets were wasted.

Copper tossed his slugs back. Blacka joined in. A bullet grazed Shim. The sting gave him a flashback. Shim couldn't handle both of the Jamaicans. So, he dived to the ground and rolled next to Mustafa.

Saif tried to exit the store. But the Jamaicans had the upper hand and the automatic fire from the Tech forced Saif back into the store. Trapped inside, Saif heard The Old Man and The Printer banging on the door. Saif fired four shots at the hostages. Sandwiched between his enemies, Saif prayed for Allah to make the fire cool.

Blacka and Copper flanked out to get a better view of their targets. Shim looked over at Mustafa. Blood leaked from Mustafa's shoulder.

Saif tried to exit again. But another barrage of gunfire met him at the door... one of the rockets connected... the impact twisted Saif's body onto the sidewalk and left him exposed.

Copper, excited about the easy target, shot and missed. Saif wasn't as careless; his hollow tip opened Copper's chest. The Rasta's life pumped from the open cavity.

"Ras clad," Blacka cried out when he saw the fatal hit. Copper was his blood.

Blacka shot in an uncontrollable rage at Saif. The bullets riddled his body. Saif flopped and jerked on the concrete. Mustafa and Shim witnessed Saif being torn from this life.

Blacka emptied his clip and kept pulling the trigger. Shim heard the clicks and sprung from his shelter. Shim let two off into Blacka's skull. And Blacka fell onto the asphalt. His brains dripped onto Ralph David.

Before Shim could regroup The Printer erupted out of the door... his SK twisted bullets across the pavement. The impact of the close range shot flung Shim's giant frame into the middle of the street. His spirit left his body.

Mustafa grabbed the bag of money and rolled under the van. By the time The Printer saw him, Mustafa had crawled into the driver's seat. The shots started again. Mustafa tucked his head below the dash and broken glass splashed onto the back of his neck. He mashed the gas pedal.

Mustafa swerved up the street. He lifted his head and regained control of the van. The light at the corner of Lee St and Ralph David turned red. Mustafa checked the on-coming traffic as he pounded on the accelerator. He saw a box truck and tried to estimate how to avoid a collision...

But the image of a young woman, holding the body of her child, distracted him. The blood of her baby dyed her white spandex red.

"Fuck me," Mustafa cursed himself.

The sound of the truck horn snapped Mustafa away from the image. He swerved and crossed over the intersection. Mustafa yanked the van onto Murphy. In his rearview a train of cop cars headed toward the murder scene.

Mustafa arrived at the warehouses. Saif's car truck hid behind the empty buildings. The pain from the gunshot and the rapid loss of blood weakened Mustafa. He fumbled for the bag of money and staggered to the car. Mustafa popped the trunk, threw in the sack of bills, and retrieved a gas can. He doused the van with gasoline.

The fire erupted as he jumped into the F-250 and put his life behind him.

CHAPTER THIRTY

1.

Ayanna sank deeper into her couch. She puffed on her second joint and flipped through the television. Her thoughts were louder than the tube. Mustafa consumed her. She didn't expect the whirlwind of emotions bought on by their connection. And then...

Breaking News flashed onto the screen...

Phaedra Jones appeared, "This is Phaedra Jones coming to you live from the West End." The screen cut to an establishing shot of the crime scene on Ralph David.

"While the majority of the Westside was at church or enjoying a quiet Sunday morning, gunshots rang out... Right here across from the West End Mall- on sidewalks generally packed with walking traffic. Leaving four dead and a 3-year-old little girl in critical condition. Cementing the terror that has taken over this community."

Cotton formed in Ayanna's mouth. Her anxiety took the lead. With no concrete knowledge of Mustafa's business dealings, her instincts told her the answers to her questions were being broadcasted on network news.

On the other side of town, Saif's kids played in front of another television- tuned to the same channel. Khadijah walked in to quiet them down. Worry had bubbled inside her. Earlier she heard the faint sounds of gunfire from her front porch. And she hadn't heard from Saif. The Breaking News grabbed Khadijah's attention.

Phaedra continued her broadcast, "It is reported that two of the Black Men dead in front of this corner store were suspected to have been involved in a quadruple homicide on Holderness back in September." Two mug shots popped on the screen. "Sources are telling us that Saifullah Syid and Hashim Ramadan have been terrorizing the West End since they were teenagers."

The tears flooded Khadijah's eyes. Her legs could no longer support her thick frame. She collapsed to her knees.

"Ya, Allah," she cried to her Lord.

"A third suspect, Mustafa Karim, is also wanted for questioning." Phaedra was once again on Ayanna's screen and Ayanna was on the edge of her seat. "The police have not made it clear as to Karim's involvement. But our sources have confirmed that in addition to the murders they have recovered a quarter-million dollars in counterfeit money and it is possible that more could still be missing."

Ayanna grabbed her phone…

Back at the corner store, on Ralph David, Phaedra finished her segment, "We will keep you updated as this story develops. And by the look of things there is a lot of information to come. This is Phaedra Jones reporting live from the West End."

Ten-second delay…

"That's a wrap," her producer called out.

Zimmer stood behind the yellow tape and watched the segment. Zimmer understood how to use the media to help crack his cases. Although, his instructions were to build his case from afar, Zimmer refused to allow bodies to pile up while the Feds decided what was important to pursue.

Agent Finn's unmarked sedan barreled onto the scene. He jumped out the car and a large vein protruded from his forehead. Zimmer expected Finn's fury. Phaedra moved to the side as Finn rushed toward Zimmer.

"What the hell is going on Detective?"

Zimmer adjusted his designer tie. "Outside of two quadruple homicides in one month... I'm not sure what you are referring to."

"I'm referring to leaking pictures of suspects in a federal investigation," Finn loved to differentiate their positions.

"Suspects that just happen to be dead on my sidewalks," Zimmer was in the perfect mood for a power struggle.

"No these would be my sidewalks, Detective," Captain Harris corrected him. Zimmer tightened his jaw; he didn't see Harris pull up. The Captain was truly his superior, and he knew better than to mouth off when he had broken the rules. "And you didn't have any authorization to give any info to the media."

Zimmer pleaded his case, "Captain.... I got streets covered in blood and automatic shells. Broad daylight... a 3-year-old in critical condition. And anybody who can tell me anything is dead... What am I suppose to do?"

Captain Harris wasn't in the space for Zimmer's games. "Follow your chain of command," Harris paused for effect, "Now, you need to collect your evidence, file your paperwork. And keep your mouth shut until you receive further instructions."

Zimmer sucked his teeth, "10-4, Captain." And he turned on his heels to exit stage left.

"Detective," Finn called behind him, "Despite what you think, we are on the same team... And some things truly are above your pay grade."

Zimmer ate the jab with silence. Being disciplined made Zimmer develop new-found interest in Agent Finn and his investigation.

2.

Mustafa pushed his SUV up the winding scenic highway. He determined it would be smart if he didn't answer his phone at all; there were too many satellites and tracking devices in the sky. The more Ayanna called, the more suspicious he became of her. After all, she was the only living person, who knew about his mountain retreat.

Mustafa hoped that the Feds hadn't somehow linked Ayanna to him. Although Ayanna and Mustafa had spent time together in the past weeks, there was nothing substantial to connect the two. Mustafa thought about surveillance... Reek and Levison. Imam Yusuf. The War on Islam. Mustafa couldn't trust anybody right now.

Mustafa pulled into the driveway of his secluded cabin. His arm still throbbed from his makeshift surgery. Mustafa took the bag of bills and buried them deep in the woods- along with his shotgun.

Every time the shovel sent pain through his arm, he thought about his brothers laid across the sidewalk. And shoveled harder.

Mustafa made wudu. The first layer he washed away was the dirt from his burial ceremony. The dirt gave way to his blood. He watched the mud and blood circle the drain and Mustafa thought about the lives he had taken. The people he had lost. He felt less righteous- like he was the one off the path... more than the drug dealers... or the rappers.

As Mustafa made his prayer, he felt overwhelmed. His actions towered over his intentions. He pleaded with Allah to forgive him for his ignorance. And to help him find his way to the *sirahtallmustakeem...*

Mustafa wondered why *the straight path* seemed to be the hardest one to follow.

CHAPTER THIRTY-ONE

1.

Mustafa used his thirty days of solitude to reflect on his life. Mustafa's way of living didn't align with the Sunnah of Prophet Muhammad; the example Allah gave him to follow. Mustafa had obeyed the ways of other men.

His mentors developed their own slant on Islam... determined what fell into the category of honorable and impure. Mustafa bought into the illusion that he had fashioned his life after the apostles of the Prophet... head-rollers like Abu-Bakr and Umar. Martyrs that fought, defended, and spread Islam.

Mustafa concluded his fight carried less nobility. He was a thief. And although, Mustafa gave his money to Zakat, charity didn't purify its means.

As he walked on to his front porch, Mustafa decided his time on the run was over. He needed to stand by his choices. Living in complete seclusion, Mustafa had no definite idea how everything panned out.

He wondered what happened to the little girl. Mustafa ate his date and visualized the young mother holding her daughter's limp, bloody body. He didn't realize the hospital released her... that a stray bullet ricocheted off a building and landed on the right side of her chest. The gunshot missed her heart and lungs.

Innocent children died from stray bullets, far too often. The little girl would only wear a scar that reminded her she was blessed to be alive. Mustafa prayed for such an outcome.

Mustafa sipped his hot green tea and wondered how things turned out with Shim and Saif. Shim was a loner; his crew was his only family. It bonded Shim and Mustafa. And Mustafa had to bear the burden of carrying Shim in his heart.

But then there was Saif. His brother. The closest to him. Mustafa watched his body being ripped a part. The image wouldn't leave his mind.

He tried to picture Khadijah- Jabril and Jennah in her arms. Children left to be raised without their father. A wife doomed for the struggle of being a widow and a single-mother. And *Dem People* liked to come and collect everything linked to a criminal. Mustafa prayed they made the proper provisions.

Mustafa pondered on the loose ends. Zimmer on the hunt. Reek on the lam. Mustafa didn't questioned what the police knew. He didn't have a TV, so he couldn't see Phaedra talk about the ongoing investigation. Or peep the secret meetings with Agent Finn and other suits reviewing files. Mustafa and Brother Abdullah's pictures connected to a slew of other suspects.

Mustafa opened his Quran. As he came across the Sura he read for Ayanna, Mustafa speculated on how her life was going. Had the police approached her? Did things work out with her mother? Surely she was familiar with what happened in The West End. He wondered how she viewed him now? Did she have a clue how much their short time together affected him?

2.

Ayanna prepared herself for her day. She wrapped her hair. The discovery of Mustafa's profession disgusted her. But in an effort to understand the mystery man, Ayanna found a real love for Islam. And though not fully converted, Ayanna attended a couple of Jummah Prayers and found a certain peace with the collective worship.

Ayanna didn't look at the caller ID when she answered her phone, "Peace... this is Ayanna."

"Peace Yani."

Ayanna recognized Mustafa's voice. She froze. She didn't believe she would ever hear from Mustafa again. Ayanna held conversations with Mustafa in her head, but now she was speechless.

"Ayanna," Mustafa called out to her.

"Yeah," she snapped back, "I'm here."

There was a moment of joint silence.

"How you doing?" Ayanna was really concerned.

"I'm aight... you?"

"Better."

"So I was thinkin'," Mustafa wasn't one for small talk.

"You lied to me," Ayanna had her own things to address.

Her abruptness came as no surprise. Mustafa expected for Ayanna to have questions. "I never told ya what I did."

"You told me you didn't harm innocent people or damage your community."

Mustafa didn't deny the truth, "Yeah... I told you dat."

"Mustafa, a little girl got shot... an innocent little girl."

"Yeah... I ain't mean for dat ta happen."

"That's the thing about that life... isn't it?" Ayanna believed him, but she refused to sugarcoat it. "You have to expect that eventually bad things will happen, Mustafa."

"You right."

Mustafa's acceptance of his wrongs made Ayanna's heart soft, but she couldn't entertain any emotions toward him. "What do you need Mustafa?"

Mustafa detected the callousness in her tone. He didn't completely buy it. So, he continued, "I'm... um... turnin' myself in on Friday, after Jummah. And I 'on't know what's gonna happen. But either way, I'd like to see ya 'fore I go."

"That's good. I'm glad you are going to man up." Ayanna took a breath and mustered her courage. "But I don't know about that... I just... There's enough going on in my life right now."

Mustafa decided not to push the issue, "I get dat."

"Mustafa..."

"Yeah..."

"You take care of yourself."

Before he responded, Ayanna hung up. Mustafa stared out into the trees. He had to face this alone. But he trusted Allah would be on his side.

"Inshallah," Mustafa said to himself.

3.

It had been over a month since Mustafa attended Jummah. The sound of the Adhan gave him solace. He entered the building and ignored the eyes that followed him.

Imam Farooq's khutbah served as background noise for Mustafa's personal prayers. He fed off the energy of the believers. Mustafa listened to the call to prayer like it was his last time, hearing its rhythm and strength. Mustafa rushed to line up next to his comrades.

Every, Allah-hu-Akbar, reverberated in his soul. He remembered that Allah was greater than everything- including his mistakes. By the time Mustafa said his Salaams, he was ready to face his fate.

And when he turned and shook the hand of the brother to the right of him, Mustafa caught a glimpse of Reek- headed out the door. Mustafa couldn't believe his eyes. He had been lost in his thoughts during the service, but how had Reek gone unseen. Mustafa thought maybe his eyes were playing tricks on him. He tried to focus on the spot where he saw Reek; his old friend disappeared.

Mustafa exited the Mosque and dropped all his money in the charity bucket. He took in the view of the congregation gathered outside. Vendors set up. They sold scarves and food. Children ran around, enjoyed the shelter of their community. Brothers and Sisters gathered and floated around in small groups. Everyone behaved like family- bound together by their beliefs. The atmosphere was festive.

Bro Abdullah strolled across the parking lot.

"As-Salaam-Alaikum," Mustafa greeted his father figure.

"Wa-Alaikum-As-Salaam-Wa-Barakhatuhu." They embraced. "So, you turnin' yourself in?" Even though they hadn't talked, Brother Abdullah stayed in the loop. And Mustafa's next move concerned him.

"Yep... jus' myself dough." Mustafa's reputation was stellar, but he wanted to reassure his mentor.

"I already know." Abdullah was still happy to hear it from Mustafa's mouth. "Don't make it too easy for 'em."

"Naw... dis dey only freebie. Dey gonna have to build da case from here... I jus' ain't in da bi'ness of runnin'," Mustafa explained his actions.

"I get that. Jus' know whateva happens, tha akhs got your back."

Mustafa couldn't bank on anybody. "I got faith in Allah. He'll make da fire cool."

"Insha-Allah." Brother Abdullah understood once inside Mustafa would need help from the Muslims. But he also realized Mustafa would have to discover that on his own.

The two men embraced and said their goodbyes. Mustafa watched Brother Abdullah walk away and his eyes roamed through the crowd. He wondered if he had really seen Reek. But then he saw her...

Ayanna…

Dressed in a bright yellow dress. The bold color contrasted the surrounding women. Ayanna's brown skin glowed against the fabric. Mustafa smiled.

And Ayanna blushed.

He couldn't believe she came to see him. After their phone conversation, Mustafa thought she was out of his life for good. But he knew Allah was the best of planners. Mustafa stared at her eyes from across the parking lot and appreciated their radiance… The beautiful details of innocence.

Mustafa mouthed, "As-Salaamu-Alaikum."

Ayanna held up two fingers and said, "Peace."

Suddenly Ayanna's eyes filled with fright. Mustafa heard the gunshot before he was hit. He turned and saw Reek staring back at him.

Two more shots and Mustafa fell to his knees. Then he toppled on to his back. And a puddle of blood formed around his face. The voices and screams became distorted around him.

Another shot. And Reek fell to Mustafa's side. Through Mustafa's blurred vision, he saw Bro Abdullah holding a smoking gun.

Mustafa felt himself slipping from this world. Ayanna crotched over him; his escaping life muted her screams. Mustafa tried to move his lips, but the sounds in his mind wouldn't form into words. His surroundings went dark… But there was no white light… Just the glow of crimson.

THE CLOSING

I remember my mother used to say, "People are too busy practicing His-lam instead of Islam... making their own rules and accepting what they want the truth to be."

I wonder if she knew it applied to her as well. She didn't want my father to have a second wife although it was his right... according to the belief they both followed.

I think at the end of the day people just want to believe what is comfortable for them to accept.

Ayanna challenged my truth. I guess, eventually, what we accept as fact has to be confronted. I pray- despite my actions- My Lord judges me on my intentions.

I, in fact, lived my life by the things I accepted as certainty. In reality, I was still that little boy sitting in front of the power light of the stereo, hoping that someone would come and save me...

In the name of Allah

The Most Gracious, The most Merciful

Master of The Day of Judgment

Thee alone do we worship and thine aid do we seek

Show us the straight path

The path of those who have received your Grace

Not of those who have gone astray.

Young Mustafa sat in front of the stereo and washed his hands over his face, "Ameen."

He stared into the crimson glow…

SUNNAH

ABOUT THE AUTHOR

Raised in Atlanta, GA, Malik Salaam was born and raised Muslim. Searching for his place in the world, he enlisted in the Navy. His inability to conform got him kicked out. But not before he discovered his talent for writing. Back in Atlanta, Salaam frequented spoken word venues and shared his well-received work on stages across the country. Eventually, he was invited to perform on networks like BET, The Black Family Channel, and HBO. His work was published in newsprint and anthologies. He performed in and co-wrote plays. His documentary, Lost in The Rubble, won film festivals and earned him positions for Congressional panel discussions. Salaam wrote, directed, and produced a feature film, Every Scar and Dimple, and a web series, Eternal. Sunnah is Salaam's third self-published body of work. Malik Salaam's goal is to be remembered as a master storyteller.